BLOOD OF WONDERLAND

COLLEEN OAKES

HarperCollins*Publishers*

First published in the USA by HarperCollins Publishers Inc. in 2017
Simultaneously published in Great Britain by
HarperCollins *Children's Books* in 2017
HarperCollins *Children's Books* is a division of
HarperCollins *Publishers* Ltd,
1 London Bridge Street, London, SE1 9GF

The HarperCollins website address is
www.harpercollins.co.uk

1

Copyright © 2017 by Colleen Oakes

ISBN 978-00-0-817542-9

Colleen Oakes asserts the moral right to be
identified as the author of the work.

Printed and bound in England by Clays Ltd, St Ives plc

MIX
Paper from
responsible sources
FSC® C007454

FSC™ is a non-profit international organisation established to promote
the responsible management of the world's forests. Products carrying the
FSC label are independently certified to assure consumers that they come
from forests that are managed to meet the social, economic and
ecological needs of present and future generations,
and other controlled sources.

Find out more about HarperCollins and the environment at
www.harpercollins.co.uk/green

This book is for Ryan, forever the good king of my heart

The Cat only grinned when it saw Alice. It looked good-natured, she thought: still it had very long claws and a great many teeth, so she felt that it ought to be treated with respect.

— Alice's Adventures in Wonderland *by Lewis Carroll*

One

The former Princess of Wonderland was lost. Leaves crunched loudly beneath Dinah's feet as she made her way through the Twisted Wood, her exhausted body groaning, her eyes taking in the maze of living trees that breathed above her. Not living in that they spoke or walked or had faces, but that they *saw* her—of this Dinah had no doubt. It was strange and unnerving, these eyes without eyes.

The trees of the Twisted Wood were taller than the Black Towers, and sometimes just as wide. The night before, Dinah had found herself not so much walking as maneuvering through them. Dinah folded her hands over her stomach—empty and ravenous, as always—and looked at the trees. Each tree was so different—some had bountiful blossoms of pink that swirled through their branches and up their trunks, some had velvety ferns that draped from weeping branches, and some were barren, with only their branches to shelter them. There were trees that grew sideways—long and low. Others were spindly towers of wavy bark, their branches shooting straight into the heavens. Some trees looked as though they had been burned; they were as black as night and their trunks gave off a faint aroma of ash. They were alive and thriving, however, as evidenced by the black and white swirled flowers that danced on the tips of their branches. It was incredible—and terrifying.

As Dinah walked, she considered how the trees knew everything. They knew that she had once been the Princess of Wonderland Palace. They knew that her father, the brutal King of Hearts, had betrayed her mere days before her coronation. He had murdered her beloved brother, Charles—once the infamous Mad Hatter—by throwing him out a window. They knew of the stranger who had sent her on her way, fleeing the palace on Morte, the devil steed, a Hornhoov whose bloodthirstiness was legendary. They knew Wardley, the love of her life, had promised to come for her. And they knew that her father was probably tracking her now.

It wasn't just Dinah's history that these trees knew—she could feel their keen awareness in her bones. These trees of the Twisted Wood knew who drew the location of the stars night after night. They knew each Yurkei and Wonderlander, those who embraced the dark and those who chose the light. Yes, the colossal trees of the Twisted Wood were aware, and that fact had both frightened and comforted her as she trekked through the wood with Morte following her, always at a distance of at least twelve paces. Farther and farther they wove their way into the wood, as the trees, always knowing, groaned and cracked around them.

Her stomach gave a loud growl and Dinah reached for her bag as she knelt on the forest floor, but not before she settled Wardley's sword close beside her. She untied the brown straps attached to the muslin and slowly laid out its contents, taking a full inventory of what she had: two white linen tunics, a belt, one black dress, eight full loaves of bread, twelve large pieces of dried bird meat, a bag of rapidly rotting berries, the remnants of her bloody nightgown, and a sharp dagger. She pulled the dagger out of the bag. It was obviously expensive, the hilt inlaid with dozens of amethysts interspersed with rich swirls of silver and gold. The black gown beside it was heavy and completely devoid of color—it was the kind of thing that Dinah would wear but Vittiore would never let drape her shoulders.

Vittiore.

Dinah ground her teeth together, gripping the dagger. No doubt Vittiore would soon be crowned queen, taking Dinah's place on the throne next to her father. It was all so clear to Dinah now, how Vittiore had always been part of the plot, always waiting in the wings to get her hands on Dinah's crown. She had long suspected that Vittiore wasn't exactly the poor child found in a sack that she claimed to be. Vittiore had been in on the plot to frame Dinah from the start. She'd been in on the plot to kill her brother, Charles. The king could never have pulled off such a coup without her willing participation. Dinah angrily closed her fist around the dagger hilt before forcing herself to calm down. She turned the dagger over in the sunlight. *Maybe I can exchange it to buy food*, Dinah thought, before she realized how silly that sounded. She would be going to no villages, no towns. Her father and Cheshire expected her to be weak, to look for help among Wonderlanders. She wouldn't. She would just disappear into the wood, forever.

I will learn to survive, she thought. *I will wait for Wardley and then we will find a boat and sail to the Other Worlds.* The thought made her weary and morose. Heavy despair seemed to hover around her, waiting for the perfect opportunity to overwhelm. If Dinah didn't keep moving, it would come for her swiftly. Her legs were sore when she pushed herself onto her feet and strapped the sword firmly across her back. Morte had fallen asleep beside her, and Dinah thought it best not to wake him. He no doubt needed the rest as much as she did, and waking an angry Hornhoov might lead to being crushed to death.

Making note of the path behind her, Dinah began wandering through the trees as she snacked on some berries. The wood seemed to go on forever in every direction.

Tiny clusters of flowers brushed her face as she pushed past a tree that spiraled in on itself, its trunk circling into the sky. The tree was weeping a frosty milk that dripped down its branches and formed a white moat around the base of the trunk. Dinah knelt beside the tree and peered into the milky substance. Tiny pink insects with gossamer wings skated over the surface, dipping their long noses into the liquid. The milk was sucked up into their bodies and distributed into their veiny, transparent wings. The white substance then gave their wings a crumbly texture, like toasted bread. At this transformation, the insects tucked their wings back and walked away, looking more like tiny lizards than the butterflies they had resembled at the start. They looked at Dinah with indifference as they strolled away into the forest.

"Incredible," murmured Dinah. She stood. The sun flashed on an unnatural shape in the distance as Dinah raised her eyes. It was tall and metallic—and not of the forest. She leaped backward, stumbled on a wide root, and fell. She scrambled for her weapon in the damp leaves as she struggled back to her feet. *I am no warrior*, she thought as her heart hammered in her ears. The metal continued to flash in the sun. Dinah advanced slowly, making her way through the trees, her sword leading the way. Trembling, Dinah clawed her way up a small embankment parallel to the flashing light to gain a better view.

The hill rose up next to a deep groove in the forest, and Dinah perched on the edge, preparing to see a battalion of soldiers waiting for her. Instead she found herself looking down into a valley . . . *of heads?* Dinah quickly counted dozens of them as she carefully made her way down the hill. Dirt rose when her boots hit the ground with a thud. The forest floor had changed—all around this particular valley, the foliage was thick and dense, with ankle-high ferns and roots tangling the ground. Here were only soft grasses that danced in the wind, their seeded tops brushing the carved heads. The heads were massive in size, most larger than Dinah's ridiculously large bed back at the palace. Some of them were propped upright, which made it appear as if the rest of their bodies were buried underground and they were simply popping up for a look around. Some of the heads lay on their sides, their lips brushed with the burnt yellow grass. One head lay completely upside down, the blunt cut of its square neck facing the sun. That head was wearing a crown, the sharp tips of the crown anchoring the head into the soil. There was something familiar about it. . . . Dinah ventured closer, making her way through the heads. She bent to look at the face and crown, her black hair brushing the dirt.

A wave of dizziness rushed over her as she realized she was looking at her father, the King of Hearts. She could tell by the crown, the same crown that encircled her father's head now, and by his heavy cheeks. Though he was made entirely of shiny bronze metal, it looked so much like her father—the same unbending will etched across his brow, the same bloodlust running through his eyes, the same hint of an ironic smile that never quite blossomed. The upside-down head stared at Dinah, its hard eyes piercing her chest. Her heart thudding, she turned away to take in the others. They were all kings and queens of some sort. She recognized several members of the royal family—her grandfathers and grandmothers, dating all the way back to those who had been present at the building of the palace.

There was Queen Millay, famous for her gracious hospitality and striking beauty. Her head lay on its side, the pearl crown on top of it covered with a creeping, soft, green moss. Next to her lay her king, King Royce. He was famous for not being faithful to his diligent queen, and for making his mistress the Queen of Hearts after Millay had died. Dinah did not see the mistress's head anywhere.

Twenty or so heads of what Dinah guessed to be Yurkei chiefs were here as well—strong, solid heads of handsome warriors carved from stone, crowned not with a piece of gold or silver, but with feathers or elaborate fabric swirls that dangled down and framed their bright, glowing eyes made of blue gemstones. Dinah found these the most haunting. The eyes of the Yurkei heads made her feel as if they were watching her as she walked along, as she touched each face and marveled at its size and beauty.

Sunlight reflected through the low clouds and sent a rippling shadow over the heads, making them look for a minute as if they were engaged in conversation—a never-ending dialogue of politics, land, and legend. Dinah was fascinated. *Who made these, and why? When? How had they transported such massive sculptures into the forest without removing the trees that surrounded them?* Dinah let her fingers run over the face of the current Yurkei chief, Mundoo, her father's enemy. The metal was warm, perpetually kissed by the sun, and it felt soothing against her cut palm. The valley was utterly unnerving and yet, somehow, also strangely beautiful.

I will take Wardley here one day, she thought, *if I can find it again.* She wasn't convinced that she could—she and Morte had twisted and wound their way through the wood not unlike the black snakes with silver eyes that she had seen in several trees so far. Together they had spiraled themselves into the deepest parts of the Twisted Wood, hoping to make their trail confusing and untraceable. How could she find her way back here, to this valley of her ancestors, who ruled when she would not? Had she been queen, would her head have one day graced this clearing? Now it would be Vittiore's. She felt the blind fury rising up inside of her, that black hunger that clawed up her stomach and wrapped its arms around her heart when she was least expecting it. *How dare they take her crown away?* With a cry, Dinah flung her sword blade across the nearest tree, hacking and jabbing until the trunk was battered and flaking. She felt the tremors vibrate up the blade and into her arm, a jarring sensation that was more cathartic than painful. Both of her hands throbbed with pain, but she didn't care.

"You killed him!" She sobbed, tears covering her face as she brought the blade of the sword down again and again against the rough trunk. "That was my crown! It was mine!" In wide arcs, she slammed her blade against the tree, the metal cutting into the wood deeper with each swipe. This wasn't swordplay, this was something else, something she had never known before. It felt glorious and dangerous at the same time, intoxicating.

Dinah continued until her arms shook with exhaustion. She angrily flung the sword away to wipe the tears off her face. Taking ragged breaths, she leaned her head against the tree, her salty tears soaking into the now-exposed virgin white wood. From its towering height, the top of the tree let out a deep groan, and Dinah watched as the bark rippled up the tree like water. Several trunks twisted accusingly in her direction.

"I'm sorry, I'm sorry, forgive me." She rested her now-bleeding hand against the raw wood, feeling the scars and notches she had left. "I'm sorry. They killed him. They took everything." Sniffling, Dinah found herself looking again at the head of her father, the way his crown was dug into the ground, the way his neck bore the blunt cut of a sword. There was an aggressiveness to this statue that the others did not share. While the other heads were resting, his position was a punishment.

An unwelcome whisper was beginning to creep up her spine, a familiar, surreal feeling. It was the same feeling that she had awakened to that night in the palace, when a stranger in black was standing over her bed. *She was being watched.* Was it the heads? Dinah stared at the statues, her eyes jumping from face to face, but she saw no movement. They were not living things, only stone and metal. Dinah slowly picked up her sword from the base of the tree and held it in front of her, both sore hands clutched firmly around the hilt.

"Come out!" she screamed. "I know you're there!" There was only silence in return as the heads stared back at her, unmoving, and the long grass waved in concentric circles around their necks. Dinah was backing up slowly, past one head, then another. There was something here—she could feel it. *Had her father found her?* Dinah spun around and her eye caught a glimpse of white moving swiftly through the high green grass. She would never make it to Morte in time. It was time to fight, time to die.

She saw the pelt of white emerge from the trees, and at first her mind wondered if her father was wearing a costume. Then she saw the claws, the black eyes, the red mouth that inspired the nightmares of Wonderland children. She heard the hungry gnashing of teeth and the licking of a fat, bloody tongue. It was a bear, and he was charging at her, letting out a roar that echoed off the metal heads and out into the wood. Dinah stood paralyzed with fear. She felt like she was in a dream, unmoving, watching death race swiftly toward her. *I need to move*, she told herself. *Move, Dinah!* Finally, her feet obeyed and Dinah sprinted toward the nearest head—an upright Yurkei chief, whose fabric crown circled lazily around his head and then looped down onto the ground. Without thinking, Dinah sheathed her sword and started her ascent, placing one foot onto his lips and pushing off the ground, grabbing hold of the chief's long nose. The eyes didn't provide anywhere to grasp, so Dinah moved sideways and pulled herself onto the man's ear by holding the tip of the large feathers that rested against his temples. A spasm of pain ripped through her hands as she heaved herself up and over the heavy swath of fabric and beads that circled his head. She leaped off the tip of his fabric crown and tumbled onto the man's head.

A roar came from below, so loud and terrifying that Dinah feared her nerves would rip apart. The bear had reached the head now. Dinah peeked cautiously over the edge. The bear was gigantic. He began pacing around the base of it, irately sniffing the ground where she had stood and pawing jagged trenches in the earth. Rising up on his hind legs, the bear's shoulders were level to the chief's eyes, just below Dinah's face. He opened his mouth and let out a bloodcurdling roar. Dinah felt a rush of hot, rancid air blow over her face and she gagged as she smelled his potent breath—a mix of decaying meat and death. It reminded her of the Black Towers.

The bear raked his huge paws down the statue's face and the terrible screech of bone meeting stone filled the air. He was a daunting creature, tall enough that his skull would brush the ceiling in her bathroom. His coat was two distinct shades of white—most of his fur was the shade of dirty cream, but the stripes that ran up from his stomach area to his visible spine were a bright, unspoiled, pure white, whiter than any garment or paint she had ever seen. His jaws snapped shut loudly as his milky eyes took in her face. Besides his massive mouth full of teeth, he also had two large fangs that rose up from the underside of his jaw. The head gave a tremor as the bear began rocking his weight against the statue. *He means to knock it over*, she thought with terror. The statue gave another tremble as the bear slammed his paws against the base and began digging in the mud around the chief's neck.

Dinah had read about the white bears of the Twisted Wood. They were sometimes passed off as myth, and many theorized that there were only a handful left. They were hard to kill, which was a shame since their pelts were worth a small fortune. Her entire body trembled as she stared down at him. The bear slammed his huge body up against the head, and it gave a violent lurch. He huffed, frustrated, and continued digging around the base before rocking the head again and again, alternating one activity for the other.

Sprays of dirt flew into the air. Dinah frantically looked around for some form of escape. The trees weren't within reach; besides, she was certain the bear could climb anything that wasn't stone. She could jump and run for it, but she was entirely sure the bear was faster. She would be dead in a matter of seconds. *Perhaps if she could entice the bear higher, she could stab its face with the end of her sword, or perhaps blind it.* That would give her the best chance.

Dinah leaned over the edge of the statue, her face low, the sword raised above her head. "I'm here!" she screamed. "Come and get me!" The bear gave her a confused look, its milky eyes focusing on her. Its jaws opened, and it let out a loud roar before charging the bottom of the statue. It hadn't taken the bait, and Dinah braced herself for impact. The statue gave another violent lurch when the bear's bulky body rammed against it. There was a moment when she thought the statue would stay upright, when it teetered on the edge of falling, but then Dinah was flying through the air and the sword dropped from her hand. She landed hard on her side and rolled into the deep grasses. She barely had time to look up before the bear was charging again. There was nothing she could do. She closed her eyes and waited for the attack.

It didn't come.

Dinah opened her eyes. The bear was only about ten feet away from her, but it was crouched and still, the fur on its back raised up into a straight line. A thud echoed behind her, and Dinah turned her head. There stood Morte, his huge spiked hooves pawing the ground lustily. The bear began to pace back and forth as he eyed Morte's ten thousand pounds of delicious horse meat, but also the bone spikes that protruded from his hooves. Even a white bear would think twice before attacking Morte. Dinah slowly crawled backward until Morte stood between her and the bear, which did not seem to notice her anymore.

The air stopped moving and for a second the valley of heads lay perfectly still, its grasses bent lazily over their stems. Dinah saw the sunlight glinting off her sword hilt. It lay next to the bear, who was swiping the ground in front of the blade with a fluid sideways motion, creating a small cloud of dirt. Morte let a long hiss of steam radiate out from his nostrils.

With a roar, the bear charged, and Morte responded in kind. They met in the middle with a terrible clash of claws and bone. In an instant they were both bleeding—the bear from its face, and Morte from his side. Together they were tangled, chest to chest. The bear reared up on its hind legs and brought its claws down on Morte's side. The Hornhoov let out a high-pitched scream as the bear sank his teeth into the horse's exposed chest, tearing off a large chunk of skin. Morte kicked the bear square in the chest before giving a great shake. Both the horse and the bear separated and charged again, tumbling to the ground in a flurry of thunder and blood. Morte landed on top this time and quickly reared himself up onto his back legs before bringing his massive hooves down onto the bear's torso. Dinah heard a sickening crunch as the weight of the hooves and the bone spikes crushed the bear's ribs and chest. Morte was stomping him to death.

The bear's massive paw swiped at Morte, tearing jagged stripes across his muzzle. Morte stepped backward, shaking his head. The bear rolled over with a roar and righted himself. His walk was unsteady, and blood flowed freely from his gut. Morte was circling the bear now, letting out angry snorts as flecks of blood flew from his mouth. The bear lumbered sideways and then raced toward his opponent again. The Hornhoov spun around, but the bear latched on to Morte's hindquarters. As the bear bit into Morte's flank and his claws tore red gashes down Morte's thighs, the massive steed let out a cry.

Unable to shake the bear by turning, Morte pushed up on his front legs. The bear lost his hold. With a strong kick of his back legs, Morte caught the bear square in the neck and sent the blood-covered beast sprawling backward.

In the sunlight, Morte's muscles pulsed and rippled with pleasure—it was obvious to Dinah that though he was injured, he was enjoying the fight—and his crazed lust for fighting filled the air with a palpable stench. He turned to reposition himself. In that moment, Dinah saw instantly why the white bear would lose. The bear was acting out of instinct, out of hunger. His need was natural. Morte saw this as a battle—his brain was strategizing as they fought, and even though the bear outweighed him, Morte was *adapting*.

The bear charged again, but this time Morte was ready. Just as the bear reached him, Morte reared up and brought the bone spikes that surrounded his hooves straight up into the bear's neck and face. The bear let out a terrible whine as Morte forced him down to the ground and delicately detached his hooves. Morte tilted his head and looked at the bear before he reared up once more and brought his hooves crashing down on the beast's chest.

Dinah looked away. The creature was now utterly unrecognizable as a tangled heap of white and red. Morte stepped back and let out a bellow. It was a deep, terrible sound, a war cry, and it chilled Dinah to the bone. Morte began galloping wildly around his kill. The bear's body shifted, and Dinah watched its exposed ribs give a final shudder before the bear surrendered his life.

Dinah stood quietly in the grass, her eyes on Morte, more afraid of him than she ever had been. Morte didn't even seem to notice her as he buried his head deep into the bear's belly and began eating. Dinah felt a wave of revulsion wash over her. She had forgotten that Hornhooves sometimes ate their kills. They were as satisfied with flesh and bone as they were with grass and grain. With her hand pressed over her mouth, she turned and walked back toward the overturned head of the Yurkei chief. Giant slashes lingered where the bear had ripped its claws across the stone. Dinah let out a long breath, suddenly aware of how close she had come to being maimed and eaten herself. This was the second time that Morte had saved her life.

After a while, Morte had eaten his fill of the bear and lay down in the grasses, nuzzling his wounded flank. Now hesitant to leave his side, Dinah raced to fetch her bag and returned quickly to the Valley of Heads. Inside, she found her old bloody nightgown. The birds in the trees began singing their shrill cries once again as she tore it into several long pieces. Head bowed, she gingerly approached the Hornhoov. He gave a soft nicker as she grew near, and Dinah took this as a good sign. Using her waterskin, she poured her remaining water over the deep cuts in Morte's flank and chest. His giant head jerked in pain, but he did not move as she cleaned the wounds using the water and her hands. As gently as she could, Dinah laid the pieces of cloth over the bloody scrapes and used her hands to press them down until the blood dried against the cloth so they would stay.

She stood and walked toward the dead bear, its chest and head nothing more than ground meat. This would take a strong stomach, she told herself, but it must be done. It was imperative to her survival that Morte trust her, understand that she knew what he was. He wasn't a pet. He wasn't hers. Brandishing the dagger she had pulled from her bag, Dinah leaned over the bear, took a deep breath, and began cutting the bear's pelt away from its body. It was grueling work. By the time Dinah was done, the sun was setting low in the east and she could see that the night would be lit by a single visible star.

Blood was smeared to her elbows, her hair matted and sweaty, both of her hands trembling with pain. Her two broken fingers throbbed, and the cut in her hand seemed to have opened again, its blood mingling with the bear's. But finally she had it—she had the pelt. It was thick and soft, the size of a large blanket, shaped into a jagged square. In a nearby creek, Dinah rinsed out the blood.

Cradling the wet pelt in her arms, Dinah brought it before Morte. The Hornhoov sniffed at the pelt and raised his onyx head to look at Dinah. She held her breath as she laid the pelt across his wide back, the trophy from his kill. Hand trembling, she reached forward and placed it just for a minute on his side. She let it linger there until Morte nipped at her arm. Her body weary in a way that Dinah hadn't previously known existed, she cleaned off the dagger, forced herself to swallow a piece of bird meat, packed up her bag, and took a long look back at the Valley of Heads. The setting sun lay heavy over the misty grasses, and the whole area simmered in a warm glow. The insect that resembled toast strutted proudly past Dinah, no doubt on its way to the milky tree that gave it life. Dinah bit her lip and began walking east as the forest descended into darkness. She took only a few paces before she heard Morte's thudding hooves behind her, cracking branches as he walked. Soon he was barely an arm's length away. The stench of death was all around him, but to Dinah, he was still a welcome smell.

Two

The days stretched into a week, or so Dinah guessed by watching the rising and setting of the Wonderland sun. She would wake in the morning and take stock of the supplies quickly diminishing in her bag.

Since they had fled the stables, Morte was actually gaining weight on Wonderland's bountiful grasses and plant life. His inky coat glistened in the sun, his muscles hard and ready. He looked healthy and strong, even with his healing wounds. Dinah was not faring as well. As she ripped into her bird meat and bread every morning, she was painfully aware that she was starving, and that each meal meant that her provisions were dwindling. What would she do when the food ran out? She had been diligent about plucking any available fruit from the trees—a Julla Tree, with its sharp and fuzzy black melons, a pink peach tree, a handful of berries. Dinah would shovel them into her mouth, her lips dark with their ripe juices. Stepping over plants and overturned logs, she walked amid countless trees stretching on forever. At night, when she settled into a thick nest of leaves or particularly soft dirt, she would set out to eat only a half loaf of her bread and always ended up eating the entire thing.

This raw hunger was something she had never experienced. She thought of all the tarts she had thrown out, of the banquets and balls where trays had been piled high above her head; lavish displays of exotic bird breasts, creatively carved pies, bubbling wineglasses, and rich fruits. *All that food, wasted; all the food she had taken for granted.* This was what she thought about when she walked, when the hunger pains became so intense that she gasped out loud. Her boots, once a deep, regal red but now covered to the tip with brown mud, crunched over dead tree branches, thick foliage, and exotic orchids.

Since the bear attack, Dinah had been more aware of how much noise she made. Hammering the tree with her sword in a moment of frenzy had no doubt attracted him. Her breathing was silent, and she tried to step softly, even when her legs felt as if they were made of iron. She tried to heighten her senses, to pay sharp attention to the wood around her. She had come within an inch of her life because she hadn't been paying attention. *It wouldn't happen again.*

Still, it was hard not to be distracted by the beauty around her. The deeper they descended into the Twisted Wood, the more breathtaking the forest became. The soft colors of the plains gave way to deep mossy greens, their fuzzy fingers reaching ever upward on towering majesties of trunks and branches. One day, as she absently had watched a red-striped otter flit in and out of a stream, she had come very close to walking off a cliff. Behind her, Morte had given a loud snort and Dinah had stopped, the tip of her boots sending a scatter of pebbles off the cliff and down into a clear river far below. Even that had fascinated her; she had never seen such translucent water or such richly colored minerals that graced the river floor. Silver layers of rock converged upon each other, giving the entire river a rippling effect, though the water's flow was quite mild.

Morte had allowed her to ride him a few times in the last few days, but only when she had grown so exhausted from walking that she found herself leaning against each passing tree to keep her balance. With an annoyed snort, he would saunter beside her and lift his leg. Dinah would climb up with a grateful sigh and feel the wave of relief that came with settling onto the already warmed bear pelt, her legs draped over Morte's neck.

One day, lulled to sleep by his easy rhythm, she was jerked awake by the feeling of a cool shadow passing over her. Dinah looked up before letting out a small gasp. The trees had converged in a thick canopy of flowering branches, interweaving with each other to create a solid tunnel of flowers. The ground beneath, deprived of sunlight, had a soft and somewhat muddy texture and was covered by a thick maroon moss. The flowers looped down through the tunnel—pinks, purples, and glossy greens, swallowing the sky. Strange white insects buzzed within the tunnel—completely rotund, they fluttered by on petite wings that barely seemed to hold them, nesting on the dewy orchid petals, waiting for their mate. Once the mate arrived, the two little creatures some-how hooked themselves together and created a warm light that glowed from both of them. Together they would float drunkenly through the tunnel.

Dinah was watching them in wonder when Morte gave a rough lurch under her—she was almost sent sprawling past his hindquarters, and would have been if she hadn't had her hand wrapped in his mane. Without warning, he was running—that pure gallop she had only experienced when she was fleeing for her life. Did he sense something? Her body tensed, hunching down, but he wasn't being chased—his steps had a lightness to them that she hadn't felt before. He was running because he could; from his mouth erupted happy whinnies. His body flowed like water beneath her, his speed unmatched by anything Dinah had ever seen. This time she was able to enjoy it—the world flying past, the greens and purples of the tunnel blending together as they raced through. His hooves barely graced the ground. Dinah felt her black hair flying behind her, her gray cloak flapping in the wind. For the first time since she had been awakened that night by the stranger's hand, Dinah allowed herself to smile, a smile that stretched into a laugh as Morte plunged farther and faster through the tunnel. *I'm flying!* she thought.

Daring to reach one hand above her head, she let her fingers trail the heads of thousands of fuchsia orchids, their swollen tongues dripping down around her. The glowing lovebugs guided their way with subtle iridescent light, bouncing off branches and flowers, occasionally whapping Dinah across her cheeks and brow. She didn't mind. She closed her eyes and enjoyed the swift wind on her face as Morte's speed intensified. The tunnel ended abruptly, with two tree trunks lying squarely in the middle of their path. Morte easily leaped over them and then began to canter at a normal speed. The air was frigid on her face, which Dinah was surprised to find soaked with tears.

Morte let her ride a bit longer that day. The more Dinah observed him, the more she understood why he had not heeded the king that day as her father had bellowed out Morte's name in a blind rage. Morte wasn't anything like a normal steed. He didn't come when called, and he wasn't to be coddled and loved, as he wouldn't give it back. Sure, Dinah gave him any apples that she ran across, but only from a distance—tossed in the air. When her father rode him into battle, he had made the mistake of thinking Morte was fighting for him—he never understood that Morte wanted to fight for himself, that he had no loyalty to the man.

Morte slept the nights away without a care, and Dinah watched him enviously as he slipped into the depths of slumber. At night, her thoughts wandered into dark places or even darker memories. Charles's body, lying broken on a stone slab. His beloved servants, Lucy and Quintrell, their throats open and bloody. The sound of the trumpets blaring from the castle and the Cards who had swarmed out of it, so ready to kill their princess. The stranger, his black figure silhouetted in front of her balcony, the way his hand had wrapped around her mouth, truly the most terrifying moment of her life. She thought about Wardley and his brown curls. Wardley, who had saved her. Wardley, who was probably in the Black Towers, black roots twisting into his body, into his brain, hollowing him from the inside out.

When she finally did fall asleep, she drifted from one

bizarre nightmare to another. The night before, Dinah dreamed that she had awakened to the sound of someone crying softly. Curiosity propelled her forward, and she came to a large clearing in the trees, where one of the Heart Cards she had killed sat on a log, softly playing a lute, a cat lounging lazily on his shoulder. Dinah had sat at his feet and listened to his weeping song as blood flowed down his chest, a crimson river creeping closer and closer to her white nightgown. She woke up screaming, covered in a cold sweat, and was unable to fall asleep until dawn began its slow rise.

Dinah's days, however, in the untamable wood were consumed with thoughts about her mother. Dinah had always tried her best not to think on Davianna. Her father had forbidden her to speak Davianna's name in his presence. In a way she was grateful to him for the excuse—it was easier than facing the raw grief, the gray wave of nothingness that would roll over her if she lingered on her feelings for just a moment. But here, she was at the mercy of her memories during endless hours of walking. The good thing about Morte was that he didn't care if Dinah wept as she walked, or if she spent an hour staring off into the hazy wood. Remembering

Davianna was a gift that Dinah gave herself—she needed to feel close to someone out here in the wilderness.

Her first memory of her mother was the tips of her fingers, trailing over Dinah's face, tracing her cheekbones and lips with absolute devotion. Her mother had loved to be touched and to touch others. She was constantly resting her hands on the shoulders of those below her—Cards, lords, ladies, merchants, but especially children, whom she adored. People were originally struck by her beauty, but the touch of her hands left them overwhelmed by her grace.

Davianna had been born the child of the Duke and Duchess of Ierladia, the largest and richest township on the Western Slope. Ierladia lay just south of Lake Todren and was the Wonderland stronghold in the North. Negotiations between Dinah's grandfather, the King of Hearts at the time, and Davianna's father, ensured her place on the throne. From the time she was born, Davianna was groomed to be the Queen of Hearts, much like Dinah.

As a child, Dinah got the distinct impression that her mother loved being queen. She wore the crown with ease. As a mother she was gentle and loving, patient with her precocious daughter who was always yanking on her crown and smudging her dresses with chocolate-covered hands. Their relationship had changed when Charles was born, but Dinah never felt neglected; rather, she saw the large amount of care that Charles took and longed to be included. And so she was. Instead of croquet or watching ostrich riding, Dinah and her mother would feed and bathe Charles, or spend the day trying to teach him to walk, or take him outside on the balcony so he could watch the ever-changing stars. Dinah didn't see her father from age three to five, when he was off fighting the Yurkei wars, and in that time she grew fiercely attached to her mother and Harris, her adviser and teacher.

Unfortunately, as Dinah grew older, she spent more time with Harris and less and less time with Charles and her mother. There were so many things to learn before one became queen, but every night Harris and Emily, her servant, had looked the other way when Dinah slipped out of her bedroom door and ran past the Heart Cards all the way to the Royal Apartments to tell her mother about her day.

Davianna would always be preparing for bed, brushing her thick black hair with her pink shell comb and staring at herself in the mirror, her tear-filled blue-black eyes staring back at her. Dinah knew she had a secret. She could see it in her eyes, in the way she held her body. Together they would climb across Davianna's heart-shaped bed and her mother would pull her close and listen as Dinah whispered to her all the tiny details of her day—what Harris wore, what Emily said, the things she had learned, how she had cried after she broke a one-hundred-year-old teapot. Every night would end with her mother whispering softly,

"Someday, my love, you'll understand everything."

Dinah's father had returned from war a changed man. He was angrier and increasingly cruel toward them both. She saw less of her mother, and when she did, Dinah was alarmed at her shrinking figure and the dark circles under her eyes. The care of Charles was taken from her and given to Lucy and Quintrell. Dinah would still occasionally visit her mother's chambers at the end of the day, but Davianna would often be sleeping, unable to take her visits, and Dinah would be sent back to her room like a child without supper.

On the eve of her ninth birthday, Dinah stumbled across a scene that she would never forget. Her daily lessons in the library had been cut short due to the sneezing of Monsignor Wol-Vore, the language tutor, and the princess found herself with a few free hours. Running happily down the hall, her pink dress in tatters behind her, Dinah made her way to her mother's apartment. The Heart Cards who normally stood guard at the queen's door were oddly absent, and the door was cracked open a few inches. As she laid her fingers on the cool knob, Dinah could hear her father's angry voice. She paused at the door.

"How dare you? You are nothing more than a common whore, lowborn trash that washed up from the sea on the beaches of Ierladia! I am the King of Wonderland, and I will not be made a mockery of. Is this how you repay me? Who is he? Tell me! I should take your head for this!"

Dinah heard the sound of something crashing—dishes, perhaps. Something hit the door with a loud thud and Dinah leaped back, afraid. She could hear her mother murmuring, attempting to calm her father.

Then: "Don't tell me it's NOTHING!" roared the man who wore the crown. Dinah heard the sharp snap of skin against skin—a slap. She desperately wanted to help her mother, but she was afraid of her violent father. Her hand lingered on the door as she heard her mother weeping behind it. Dinah walked back to her chambers, a coward.

She never told anyone about that day, not even Wardley. It was strange to think of it now, as she stepped over root after root, the muscles in her thighs clenching with fatigue. A tiny stream crossed in front of them, and Dinah stopped to fill her waterskin. Morte lapped at the water, and Dinah sat down on the muddy bank to rinse off her sore feet. The tinkling of the stream had a lulling power, and Dinah raised her face to take in the warm sun, resting for just a minute, just one more memory.

Her mother had died on a winter afternoon, when huge mounds of pink snow were piled high against the Iron Gates outside the palace, and inside everyone was trying to stay warm. Her illness had been violent and sudden. One day, Dinah's mother had been there, her face thin and worried, but alive. The next she was lying in her bed, drenched with sweat so hot that it steamed in the cool air. Her lips, once the color of a ripe fig, were blue and withered, and her eyes were somehow gone already. They looked past Dinah, as if the queen were seeing someone else. The White Fever had raged through Wonderland proper that year, a quick illness that turned a person's nails white before it swiftly delivered them to the grave. Although it was curious that no one in the palace had gotten it, aside from her mother.

Dinah hadn't been allowed to touch her mother, or even to go near her bedside. She stood sobbing in the doorway, Harris's arms wrapped firmly around her, holding her back, as she watched her mother's body convulse and twist in pain. Charles was not allowed in the room, and the king was nowhere to be seen as Davianna took her last breath, her eyes finally trained on Dinah as she whispered her goodbyes, her body shaking with the effort.

"Dinah, oh my wild girl. You so are smart, just like him. Be gentle, my dear, take heart. Be a good queen. Take care of your brother."

Dinah wept, her fat tears dripping off her chin. "I will, Mother. I will. I love you. I love you."

The hint of a smile brushed across Davianna's face. "I love you too. . . ."

The conversation had exhausted the queen, and it

wasn't long after that she fell into a heavy sleep, never to wake again. The rising of her chest slowed until it ceased. The queen was declared dead. Her father, her servants, Harris, everyone who had known her mother, wailed. Even Cheshire's dark eyes filled with clever crocodile tears. The Cards came and went; a priest, wearing long red robes covered with hearts, rang a tiny silver bell outside her window. Another bell from somewhere down below rang in return. Suddenly bells were ringing throughout the kingdom, and the sound of them rose up through the courtyard and in through the open window as a swirl of pink snow rested on her mother's lips.

Dinah screamed and flailed in Harris's arms when the thin ruby crown was removed from her mother's head. The priest held it over open flames until the crown glowed a dim red, as if lit from within. She realized with a start that it was a precautionary measure, to cleanse it from the fever. He walked over to Dinah as he blew on the crown to cool it.

"The queen is dead. Long live the future Queen of Wonderland." He placed the crown on her head, the heat of it scorching the tips of her ears. Harris carried her out of the room, and as he turned, Dinah was given one last glance at her mother's face, her beauty siphoned away by death.

Taking a cue from her father, Dinah had built a wall around that memory, thick as stone and impregnable to wandering thoughts. But here, in the depths of the Twisted Wood, it had been so easy to remember. She could smell the putrid air of the bedchamber, could see the fear in Harris's eyes as the hot crown was laid on her head.

Dinah wiped her eyes as she pushed her blistered feet into the cool stream. The relief was instant, and it occurred to Dinah that she could possibly stay here forever, in this tiny lovely part of the wood where all the trees were white and the huge dark blue and deep green veiny leaves stretched out over the ground. *But she couldn't. Not yet.* After a few moments, Dinah pulled her feet out of the stream, delicately wrapped them with the remaining strips of linen, and pushed them back into her boots, now instruments of torture. She watched silently as a fiery red hawk danced and dipped over the horizon, such a thing of beauty. She looked hopefully over at Morte, wishing he would lift his leg and have mercy on her. He did not, but rather stared off into the distance, his massive black head tilted with interest.

"I guess we'll be walking, then," groaned Dinah. It was nice to hear a voice—any voice, even if it was her own. They continued walking northeast. Her march to starvation, as Dinah had begun to think of it, dragged on.

The tracking hawk continued to circle lazily overhead.

Three

All day Dinah had felt strange. She had just eaten her last loaf of bread and there were only a few pieces of bird meat left. A creeping feeling made its way from her spine to her forehead. She convinced herself that it was just the sinking feeling of having no more food. Her time was up—she would either need to learn how to hunt or begin eating only fruit that she could find along the way, but that wouldn't sustain her for long.

Dinah was losing weight rapidly—already she had tightened her belt loop two notches, and when she had splashed her face in the stream that morning, she was shocked at how thin her face looked, how tired. Her hair was a raggedy tangle that would probably take years to work itself out, and her skin was marked with dozens of small cuts from thorny branches. The cut on her hand was healing well, but her two broken fingers still ached whenever she put pressure on them. The shocking thought that she might not survive this ordeal washed over her like a cold wave. *I cannot die from something as simple as a lack of food*, she told herself.

That day she kept a very sharp eye out for things that looked edible. She found a Julla Tree, but most of its spiky fruit had gone rotten. Dinah managed to grab three fruits that were edible and stashed them in her bag for the following day. She found a strange plant in the ground that sprouted something similar to the cabbage they ate at the palace. Tentatively, she rested a leaf on her tongue only to spit it out immediately. It was bitter and numbed her tongue, and she quickly rinsed her mouth out with water. *I'll die from poisoning much faster than starvation*, she thought.

The wood was filled with such fascinating and terrifying plants: huge rubbery vines that gave a shiver when she passed, and when she touched them, they released a puff of sparkling yellow powder; tubal roses that grew long instead of wide, whose petals collapsed inward when the sun set; carnivorous plants that feasted on small rodents—and once attempted to bite Dinah's ankle and would have broken the skin if she hadn't been wearing boots. There were thousands of ever-changing plants and flowers woven among the trees—those trees, always knowing—and none of them to eat. *Damn it.*

Grumbling to herself while ignoring the sharp pain in her stomach, Dinah walked on, watching the blazing sun creep from west to east as dusk settled in like a thick blanket. Without warning, she found herself in a small clearing, marked by a unique tree that had small, perfectly round holes drilled into its impossibly wide trunk. Dinah walked up quietly to inspect the tree, noting that it was at least twice the width of her bedchambers. She padded slowly around the smooth trunk, letting her hand linger on its surprisingly glossy surface. The bark had the texture of marble. It shimmered in the setting sun, the light playing across it like a warm ember. Dinah watched with amazement as rays of sunlight shot through the tree, and suddenly it hummed with life, as if lit from inside. The tree was transparent and filled with a frozen golden sap. She could see everything inside it—every fiber, every bubble of air. This was an amber tree, something she had only seen in her picture books, valuable because they were so rare. Once found, they were immediately hacked down and turned into jewelry, furniture, and hand railings for the wealthy. The base of her tea table was made of this rare amber wood.

Dinah ran her hands over the trunk. It was so beautiful it took her breath away—why would anyone ever chop it down? There was so much more beauty in a living tree than a pendant wrapped around some noblewoman's neck. The tree pulsed with warmth that Dinah suspected didn't come from the sun, but rather from inside the tree. Her fingers trembled with the knowledge that its texture was changing underneath her skin. Whereas before it had felt like cool marble, it now was soft, like the jams she spread on toast. When she pulled away, her hands were covered with a dark, drippy syrup the color of molasses. Without thinking, she licked it. After weeks of stale bread and dried bird meat, the syrup was heavenly—rich and sweet, the best thing she had ever tasted. She licked her hands dry, covering her face in syrup, and went back for more until she felt sluggish with the sugar, drunk on this rush of goodness. She stumbled away from the tree past Morte, who had also been licking the trunk.

Dinah was wiping her hands on the damp grass when she looked up in surprise, her eyes catching a strange form in the trees. There was a house in front of her. Dinah leaped back in shock, her hand on her sword hilt. How had she not noticed it? The house sat snugly between two trees, their roots twisting up through the roof. It reminded her of the Black Towers, of that root twisting itself into her mouth, up her nostril. . . . Dinah heaved up the syrup onto the ground, the thick sludge puddling at her feet. Afterward, to her relief, she felt much better without its weight sitting in her stomach.

Dinah gaped at the house as she crouched behind the liquid tree. There was no visible light coming from the house, no candles flickering in open windows, no guards against the approaching night. Morte flattened his ears back against his head and gave a loud huff. Dinah felt that familiar dread that had plagued her all day. While longing to plunge back into the safety of the wood, Dinah found herself drawn to the man-made structure. It had been so long since she had seen anything related to humans, and she longed to run her hands over the walls, to feel timber and bolts, blankets and cups. Also, she reasoned, there might be food in the house, something she could not ignore.

Scrambling on her knees, Dinah found a small rock and threw it at the door. It bounced off with a loud thud and landed beside an empty bucket. Dinah waited a few minutes, but nothing happened, other than the wind tossing the branches of the trees overhead in a lulling whoosh. She drew her sword and approached cautiously, on silent feet. Dinah crouched low beneath the window and raised her head to peer through the beveled glass. She could see nothing through the thick glass, but she could sense that everything was still. With a deep breath, she turned the door handle. The door swung open and rocked on its hinge. Dinah stepped inside. The house was one large circular room with a beautiful high-vaulted ceiling and a dirt floor. On the right, an unmade bed had been overturned and books were scattered about, their pages flapping in the wind. At the front of the room sat a cold fireplace, cozied up to a sitting area that featured a well-worn rocking chair resting against the wall. A blanket had been ripped to shreds and tossed about the room.

To the left was a kitchen but it had been recently ransacked. Milk dripped from an overturned jug onto the floor, where a basket of food had been tossed aside. Hunger making her impulsive, Dinah raced toward it. She pushed past the overturned table, stepping over the blue-and-white-spotted teakettle smashed on the floor. She didn't care—all she saw were two loaves of bread, some onions, carrots, and what looked to be a burnt husk of thick deer meat. Ravenous, Dinah threw these things into her bag as the sun dipped behind the cottage, filling the room with a shadowy light. She gnawed at the bread. *Who had been here? Yurkei? Had an animal gotten in—a wolf? Something worse?* Dinah looked around. No. The chaos seemed a little neat for an animal, a little too intentional. What animal would leave food but rip pictures off the wall and flip a bed over?

Morte gave a nervous whinny from outside and pounded the ground with his heavy, spiked hooves. The dishes inside rattled. Dinah took one last glimpse around the kitchen before ducking out of the round house. She said a silent thanks to whoever baked this bread and grew these onions as she made her way behind the house, back into the wood. Morte dutifully followed behind her before they both stopped short. There was a long field that stretched hundreds of feet behind the garden, and a body was there, lying facedown in the dirt. He had been quite large but obviously strong—huge muscles, still as stone, looked as though they had been carved out of his back. He wore a floppy hat and a lavender linen tunic, his feet bare and dirty. *A farmer,* Dinah thought, pressing her fingers across her trembling lips. Broken jars of the amber tree syrup littered the ground around him. Dinah felt all the air rush out of her lungs as she comprehended what she was seeing. Out of the man's back arched a long arrow. It nestled between his great shoulder blades, a small blotch of blood surrounding the entry point. He had bled out from the front, the ground stained a deep red all around him. The blood was still wet, but it was cooling quickly and becoming one with the sticky syrup, a sickening, swirling mixture of red and amber.

The fact that this hadn't happened long ago alarmed Dinah, but not as much as the red blown-glass heart that topped the end of the arrow. She had seen these arrows before, adorning the backs of many Heart Cards that guarded the outer gates of the palace. She stood, the world spinning around her. It wasn't the Yurkei who had been here. The Cards had found her. Dinah swung the bag around her back and ran straight toward Morte. "Up!" she barked. Her panic was evident and for this he didn't hesitate, lifting his leg as she neared him. Dinah stepped without fear onto his spikes and vaulted herself onto his back, her legs curling around his massive neck.

From what she could tell, the tracks of the Cards (huge, impossible not to notice once she was looking) were heading north, and so she turned Morte east. From there, they ran. Her heart thudded in her ears as Morte raced through the ever-blackening wood. Farther and farther in they dashed, making an incredible noise, yet what chance did they have not to? Dinah could barely see, but Morte seemed to have perfect night vision—he easily navigated branches and deep holes in the earth without trouble. Every few seconds, she would glance back, praying that she wouldn't see a white Hornhoov emerging from the darkness. They had made it a few miles from the house when she heard the first faint shouts and clinking of armor. Fear surrounded her and made it hard to think. The sounds seemed to be coming over a dark ridge in the distance.

Tears welled up in her eyes and her hands shook as she clutched Morte's mane, turning him around, racing away. As he ran, the sun disappeared over the Yurkei Mountains and all was black. The Twisted Wood became nothing more than shadows, an inky shade of trees and branches. Dinah could barely see Morte's head in front of her as he dived through the trees, straining to outpace the growing sounds of horses and men. The cacophony was coming from all sides now, so foreign and abrasive to her ears after so much silence. Morte's arrival desecrated the quiet wood, violating the peace of the trees, the hum of the insects. She couldn't see where her pursuers were, but they were getting closer—and there was nowhere to run where they wouldn't hear Morte crashing through the brush.

Dinah drew her sword and the ring of metal echoed

through the trees. She wouldn't be able to fight through many of them—any of them, maybe—but she would not be taken to the Black Towers. She would force them to kill her, and she would try her best to kill her father. That was her only purpose on this night; if this was going to be the way it ended, so be it. She would avenge her brother, his keepers, and lastly her mother, slowly killed by her father's neglect and cruelty. Dinah sat still and held her breath for a moment. Then her father's voice carried through the darkness, commanding his troops, the sound sending a dagger of fear straight through her.

"She's here! Bring her to me, dead or alive. A lifetime's worth of wages and a position in the court will be given to the Card who finds her. Do your duty and avenge your innocent prince! His blood will not be in vain!"

The voice stopped Dinah cold—Morte as well. They stood perfectly still as the roar of soldiers echoed all around them in the darkness. They were surrounded. A leaf crackled directly behind Dinah, and she heard deep breathing.

"Hide," whispered a voice in the darkness. "If you want to live, don't fight. Hide."

Dinah didn't need to be told twice—or have time to consider the source of her advice. She quietly dismounted Morte and bid him to follow her into a densely leafed area of the trees, stumbling many times over things she could not see. Something slithered over her boot and she forced herself not to scream. It was a consuming darkness. *The stars must be on the other side of the sky tonight*, she thought, *hiding from this terrible noise.* The sounds of the Cards were all around her—the violent breaking of tree branches, the clanking of cups against thighs, horses pawing the ground, and a singular sound that chilled her blood—the thundering sound of another Hornhoov.

She stood still, considering how best to hide—and to hide Morte. She looked over at him through the night but could see almost nothing—the black of his coat blended effortlessly with the trees and night. *I have to disappear*, she thought. *Disappear into the night. The dress.* Moving as quickly as she dared, Dinah untied the flaps on her bag and rummaged through it, her hands feeling for the thick, heavy fabric. When it seemed she had touched everything in her bag except for what she needed, Dinah's hand felt it. She pulled out the dress, unfurling it against the starless night. Dinah could barely see her hand in front of her face, let alone the pitch-black fabric of the dress. Dropping her sword to the ground, she pulled the dress over her head. It slipped over her easily, the ends of the dress brushing the ground. Reaching back, she felt that the dress collar was lined with a hood. Dinah pulled the black wool over her dark hair and face. It was long enough to cover everything, and the fabric reached her chin. She pulled her hands into the sleeves so that they would not show and inched up next to a particularly wide tree, leaning into the trunk.

The voices were almost on top of her now—they would be on her in seconds with their swords and horses and torches. She looked over at Morte, who stood as still as she was, white steam hissing out of his nostrils. It was taking every inch of his control not to leap into the fight. Dinah reached out and felt for his nostrils. She gently and carefully laid her hand over his muzzle. Her voice shaking, she murmured, "Still . . . still. . . ." The steam stopped and Morte knelt on the ground, becoming one with the thick foliage around him. Perhaps the animal knew he could not win this fight, not tonight, not while he was still recovering from the bear attack. Either way, Dinah could no longer see him. She pressed her face and body up against the tree and waited for them to come. Quivers of fear crawled up from her legs and infested her chest. Her knees felt weak. She clutched at her heart.

"Don't move," whispered the same voice from before. Was it above her? "Don't move, don't breathe, and the Cards shouldn't see you." Dinah froze, a black statue in the wood. She closed her eyes as the Cards swarmed around them. Several Cards trampled right past her—it sounded like one almost tripped over Morte before he suddenly changed direction and veered to the right. *He should be thankful to be alive*, she thought, *as that would have ended in his very gruesome death*. Two brushed past the tree she was leaning against, and Dinah clenched her hands inside the sleeves to keep from fainting. Unable to raise her head for fear of being seen, Dinah kept her eyes glued to the ground. She could see nothing except the occasional flash of a torch as it was waved in the darkness, the wood swallowing the light in their vast space.

The voices of the Cards flowed past the trees. "She was here!" "I heard her, Your Majesty!" "She's over there!" The echo of the Cards bounced through the wood, making it very hard to tell where each man was—and she could see that the Cards were disoriented and scattered. They were unaccustomed to the trees, to the starless night. To Dinah's horror, she felt the earth shake beneath her feet and heard the singular plodding with which she had grown so familiar. She dared to raise her face a few inches. The white Hornhoov carrying her father had entered the trees, with Cheshire's sleek stallion following behind him. Her father sat proud and furious atop a female half the height of Morte but still gigantic. He carried a torch, so clearly visible in the darkness that surrounded the rest of the Cards. He wore his red armor, a black heart slashed boldly across the chest. The gold of his crown glinted in the firelight, his eyes lit up like flames. He held the reins on the Hornhoov in one hand and his Heartsword in the other, ready to kill. He seemed to stare right at Dinah, right through her. Beside him, Cheshire sat with his dagger clutched loosely as he scanned the wood, his black, catlike eyes searching each tree, his purple cloak draped over the flank of his steed.

The Hornhoov turned her head in their direction, and the king began thundering toward them. Dinah clutched the tree, pressing her face against it, fearing that her heart would actually explode.

"Stay still," ordered the voice. Dinah froze as her father's Hornhoov walked closer to them, his torch only lighting the few feet in front of him. Carefully, she raised her head and saw her father in the darkness, his face a mask of righteous fury. The king looked confused, as though he were unsure of what he was seeing. He was close enough that she could make out the sweat on his brow and smell the stink of drink clinging to his skin. She was sure he could hear her heart, which thudded with enough power to shake the tree.

Her father climbed off the Hornhoov and began making his way toward the clump of trees where Dinah was standing. Hatred flooded over her fear, and she felt an intoxicating rush of fury circle up from inside her gut. *He killed Charles*, she thought. *And I will kill him now, a shadow in the darkness. Yes, my king, come ever closer.* Moving as slowly as she could, Dinah reached for her sword, her eyes trained on his neck, the only open spot in his armor. Suddenly there was a loud crash from the wood behind her.

"There!" yelled a soldier from a distance away, "I heard something over there! I think it's her!" The king's face distorted with pleasure, and he vaulted back onto the Horn-hoov, turning her in the direction of the sound. Cheshire followed, giving a backward glance at the seemingly empty valley before raising his dagger menacingly and following the king. The king's Hornhoov kept trying to turn back—it could obviously smell Morte—but Dinah's father simply yanked the reins and dug his spiked heels in.

"Go, you blasted creature! Find her!" Together they galloped off into the brush, the light from his torch dimming to a dull candle in the darkness.

"Go . . . ," snapped the voice, and then Dinah heard the sound of a body dropping down from the tree above.

"Who are—"

"No time!" snapped the voice, distinctly male, some-how familiar. "Yeh, go! I'll lead them south. Quickly, for they will surely come back here." He was as invisible as she was, a hulking, dark shape in the trees. Dinah flung the bag around her, climbed onto Morte's back, and strapped the sword across her shoulders. She leaned forward and pressed herself against his black coat, becoming invisible once more. Black on black, a shadow at midnight.

"Quietly now," she whispered to her giant steed. Morte seemed to understand as they headed east, his hooves gently kissing the earth. They moved far away from the roaming Cards, deeper and deeper into the night, until the sounds of her father's army were no more. They walked quietly for hours, and Dinah noted that the flat floor of the forest was now increasingly sloping upward, harder and rockier. Hornhoov and rider moved soundlessly through the trees until Dinah spotted a small rock outcropping perched upon a narrow ridge overlooking the forest. Strategically, it would be a great place to watch for the approaching Cards, and besides, the trembles in her legs reminded her that they should go no farther. Without a word, she slipped off Morte and collapsed against the rocks, exhausted from her ride and from the all-encompassing fear. Morte knelt behind the rocks next to her and fell quickly into slumber, leaving her alone with the night sky.

Comforted by the fact that she didn't think her father's army could sneak up on them in the dark—or find them in the dark, for that matter—Dinah let her eyelids flicker closed once, twice, and then she surrendered to her voracious exhaustion. She dreamed of a deck of cards on a glass table, being played by a black glove. The hand was detached from an arm, and tiny flecks of crimson dripped across the faces on the cards as they were revealed. Hearts. Spades. Diamonds. The king. The king. The king.

Her eyes opened again in the early dawn and she woke drenched in a feverish sweat, unsure of what had awakened her so suddenly. Then she heard the click of a boot in front of her and felt a cold steel blade pressed firmly against her neck. Trembling, she raised her eyes, her black braid brushing the tip of her sword. A Spade stood before her, his massive frame blocking the sun.

"Morning, Princess."

Dinah flew backward, knocking her spine against a rock. Picking up a handful of loose dirt, she flung it at the Spade's face and felt the ground for her sword. The Spade gave an annoyed cough.

"You won't be finding that now, Yer Highness." The Spade raised his other hand, which held Dinah's sword. He had two swords and she had none. "Yeh know, it's not very princess-like to throw dirt."

Dinah paused a second before slowly inching herself toward the Spade, hoping to scramble over the rock to where

Morte lay snoring on the ridge above. *Why is he still sleeping? Curse that lazy beast!* As she moved forward, his blade slid coolly against her throat. She stopped moving.

"Don't be calling that monster of yours. I just want to talk to yeh, that's all."

Her heart galloped wildly in her chest and Dinah glanced frantically around for the rest of the king's men. "Where are the others?"

"Ah, them. I left them behind." The Spade stepped forward into the light and Dinah gave a loud gasp.

"You!" She recognized the Spade instantly—his dark gold eyes, his grizzly gray hair, the tiny black heart tattooed under his right eye—mostly because of the shallow two-inch scar that ran down his left cheek. "I know you."

The Spade smiled and drew his sword lightly across the mark. "Yes, yeh know me. You gave me this, you may remember, back in the palace when I dared to pluck a silly wooden toy from yeh. Yeh slapped me with a big ring? A big ring for a spoiled princess."

"It wasn't my toy. It was for my brother."

The Spade grimaced. "He won't be needing that much

now, will he? Wings might have helped more."

Dinah let out an angry scream before she feinted left, twisting past the sword, and managed to grab the Spade's black breastplate. He roughly shoved her backward with one hand. She tumbled in the dirt. He was so *strong*. She flung a rock at him, which bounced off his armored chest.

"Do not speak of my brother, you filth!"

The Spade peered at Dinah with fascination. "Just as spirited as I remember yeh! Now shut that privileged mouth and listen to what I say. I'll need yeh to promise that you won't try to run from me, otherwise I might have to give you a matching scar. And unlike me, you aren't pretty enough to make it charming."

Dinah sat back, her legs collapsing underneath her. The Spade wiped his face with his sleeve and tossed Wardley's sword into a nearby bush. He then dropped his sword down to waist level, his keen eyes never leaving Dinah's face. Her eyes met his and there was a moment of silence where they stared at each other. He stroked his goatee, peppered black and gray.

"I'm here to aid yeh. You can't make it very much longer

without my help. Yer father and the Cards will find yeh. Maybe not today, maybe not tomorrow, but they will. And when they do . . ." The Spade pursed his thin lips and drew his finger across his neck. "Your father is a king entirely without honor." His eyes focused sadly upon the wood behind her.

Dinah stared at him, not understanding what he was saying. *He wants to help me?* She followed his eyes to the side, giving the impression that she was considering his speech before bolting off to the right. She almost made it past the edge of the boulder and opened her mouth to yell for Morte but before she could, the Spade caught her around the waist and flung her roughly to the ground. Dinah's still-healing fingers vibrated with pain, and the Spade reached forward and boxed her on her right temple, which left Dinah's head spinning. Blood seeped into her ear.

"Oh, fer gods' sake . . ." The Spade picked her up and easily propped her back underneath the rock overhang. "We'll try again. My name is Sir Gorrann. I've been a Spade in the Cards service for thirty years, and I am here to help yeh, if you will just settle down and stop behaving like a wild bear, damn yeh." Dinah was having trouble breathing, and the world spun around as her hearing slowly returned. She was unsure of what was happening. He gave a loud sigh.

"It makes me unhappy to treat yeh so, but until you stop tryin' to run, it'll just be beatin' after beatin'." He settled down next to Dinah on a tree stump and pulled off his black gloves, flexing his hands. She laid her forehead against the ground, her hands curled protectively over her head.

"I can't . . . I can't . . . think."

"Aye, you've never been hit before, have yeh? More reason that you need help to survive. I can teach you many things, Princess. How to cover a track, how to fight, how to find food."

"I know how to fight," mumbled Dinah.

"No, yeh don't. That handsome stable boy might have taught yeh a few things, but fighting wasn't one of them."

"Wardley?" At his mention, everything in the world seemed to stop. "What do you know about Wardley? Is he alive?"

"Ah, now yeh want to talk." The Spade dusted off his black tunic, adorned with a glossy black Spade symbol. "Tell you what, Princess—I'll make yeh a deal. Yeh stop trying to run, and make sure that horse of yers doesn't impale me on one of his bone spikes, and I'll tell yeh everything yeh want to know about Wonderland and what's happened since yer . . . departure."

Dinah blinked in the rising sun, her eyes trained on the Spade's face. "I remember you. You left the gate open that night. You could have shut it, but you waited. I saw you. You paused . . ."

The Spade gave a quick nod. "That I did. Now, we best be on the move. If we stay here, the king's Cards will be on us in less than an hour."

"How do you . . . ?"

The Spade gave a low whistle, and a reddish-brown mare approached on gently trotting feet. Dinah frowned. Morte would definitely not come if she whistled.

"Answer me this, traitor: Why are you not with the king?"

The Spade gave a snicker as he mounted the mare. "Let's just say that I have my own interest in helping yeh.

But that's not for yeh to worry about yet. Before I'll answer any questions, I need yeh to straddle that black thundercloud and ride."

Dinah climbed unsteadily to her feet. "How long?"

"How long fer what?"

"How long until you answer my questions?"

The Spade gave a laugh. "I'll answer one question each time the sun sets. Now, we really must go." He had her just where he wanted her, she was sure of it, but what else could she do? She could no more stop breathing than turn away from knowing Wardley's fate.

"How is it that you know what they are doing if you aren't with them?"

The Spade had already begun riding into the trees, which were looking ever more whimsical on this side of the Twisted Wood. "I know because I'm the king's best tracker, or at least I used to be. They are tracking yeh even now, and after yer close call last night, I'm sure yeh know what that means. They will rush in like water, surrounding yeh from all sides. The darkness won't hide yeh again, not with the trees thinning out the farther east we go."

Dinah wiped her face on the heavy black dress. "That was you. You told us to hide."

"Aye. And if I hadn't, yeh would be headless right now, since yeh were determined to fight an entire army for one single moment of revenge. I hope I can teach yeh to think about the consequences of yer actions, to control that fury."

"My father murdered my brother."

"Not the first, I imagine, to be wronged at the hands of the king, vengeful bastard that he is, but that's a discussion for another time. We must move."

From the depths of the Twisted Wood below, she thought she heard the faint blast of a trumpet. They were still looking for her, and if she stayed, they would find her. The Spade was right. There was no choice. She pushed her hair back from her face and glowered at the Spade. "Fine. Let me get Morte."

"Oh, is that his name? He's a ripe, ferocious animal that one. I've seen him in battle. Killed a dozen Yurkei right in front of me."

"You should ride him. He loves new riders."

The Spade chortled. "I don't think I'll be doing that today, Princess."

"Don't call me princess anymore," she snapped quietly. "My name is Dinah."

He tipped his head in her direction as his brown steed disappeared under a clump of mossy green trees. Dinah stood still for just a second, letting the breeze rush over her. There was a new chill in the air, and she realized with a start that from the top of the rock outcropping, she could see the faintest outline of the Yurkei Mountains, once far on the horizon. The trees in the valley below groaned hungrily in the breeze, and she saw several of them reach out to welcome the clean, frigid air. In the azure sky above, a red-feathered hawk dived again and again into the wood, searching for food, spiraling with deadly efficiency as it sailed above the trees. Its feathers rippled like fish scales, and she watched as the flaming colors danced over its small form.

Something silver winked from the bird's neck in the morning light. She squinted. *A collar.* Dinah felt her breath catch in her throat. That was a tracking hawk. It was not hunting rodents, it was hunting *her*.

Dinah threw the filthy wool cloak over her shoulders and began to climb out of the rocky nest. Morte slumbered above, his spiked hooves pressed out in front of him. Dinah cleared her throat. He did not stir. She coughed again, loudly this time. One of his black marble eyes popped open, and he watched Dinah as she began to weave her way up the forest trail, following the Spade. She walked for several minutes before she spotted Sir Gorrann up ahead, his horse meandering through the wood as the Spade hummed a soft tune under his breath. He gave Dinah a smile as she came up the path behind him.

"I think I saw a tracking hawk."

"Indeed you did. His name is Bew, and he belongs to one of the king's trackers, Sir Fourwells."

"Will he find us?"

"Not now that yer with me." The Spade raised his eyes, taking in the trees and the increasingly rocky landscape. "We won't have to flee long. I doubt the king will lead them out of the Twisted Wood. If they don't find yeh here, they'll probably head up to Ierladia, to pay a very unpleasant visit to yer mother's family."

"Why wouldn't they follow us?"

The Spade leveled her with an exasperated gaze.

"Because we're getting close to Yurkei territory, and because your father isn't comfortable 'round these parts."

The Spade blinked in the sun before reaching down and yanking a tall piece of wheatgrass to put into his mouth. "Yer just as smart as they say." The ground gave a slight tremor as Morte appeared at the end of the trail, his colossal body reflecting the bright sun as he climbed toward them with alarming speed. Sir Gorrann's mare took a step backward, almost tripping over an overturned branch. Even she knew better than to trifle with a Hornhoov. Sir Gorrann's face paled.

"Gah, he is massive! Can yeh control him?"

Dinah gave a shrug and picked up a stick to fling angrily into the trees. "Not really. I wouldn't touch him if I were you."

Before she could release the stick, the Spade's hand,

nails black as soot, clamped onto her wrist. "No throwing sticks. No touching anything that yeh don't have to. Don't throw, don't kick, don't shuffle yer feet or run yer hands along the trees. It's going to be hard enough covering his tracks"—he motioned at Morte, who was munching on some tiny yellow flowers that popped open like bubbles when he crunched them—"without yeh leaving yer scent and marks everywhere. Yeh might as well have left a royal red carpet behind us!"

They walked until the sun was high in the sky, breaking for a quick lunch beside a stream. The Spade pulled some dried meat and a small wrapped cheese out of his pack. Dinah's mouth watered at the sight of the cheese, but she forced herself to look away and appear happy with her stale bread. She didn't want anything from this man.

"Give me yer boots," he ordered gruffly, and Dinah obeyed. He rinsed them out in the stream, taking care to scrub the soles with diligence. He handed them back to her. "Step lightly. Try not to tramp around the wood making as much noise as possible like yeh've been doing." Dinah watched in fascination as the Spade fastened two low-hanging pine branches to his belt so they dragged behind him. He pointed to the stream. "You and the horse need to walk in the stream fer the next few miles. This is where I plan on losing them fer good."

It was easier said than done. Getting Morte to follow her into the ankle-deep stream was incredibly difficult. Eventually he was lured in by the large piece of meat Dinah had grabbed in the farmer's house. Morte didn't like the water on his spikes, although it was clear they needed it—swirls of dried blood colored the water when he finally stepped in. They followed the stream as it flowed uphill. Everything flowed uphill now—the land, the flowers, the plants. Dinah quickly sweated through the heavy black dress. Walking in the stream was difficult. Several times she stumbled. Her ankle caught on seaweed, rocks, and much to her horror, a silver-and-rose-striped snake. After a few miles, the Spade ordered her to leave the stream and walk in only her socks. He shuffled behind her, erasing their footprints. Every once in a while the Spade would lick his finger and hold it in the air or stop and tilt his head, listening for something inaudible to her own ears. Then he would correct their tracks, step by step. At one point, he made Dinah climb a tree only to climb back down on the other side. She protested loudly, until the Spade drew his sword. She grumbled all the way up and all the way back down as Morte watched her with amusement.

Several times Dinah would begin to talk only to be shushed by him, and once, without warning, the Spade pushed her down into a bush, laying his body on top of hers, followed by several branches and brush. Dinah let out a shriek and pushed against him with all her might, fearing he wanted to defile her in a way she had only read about, but his hands had only cupped her mouth. Dinah struggled until she saw the red shimmer of the tracking hawk above, dancing in and out of the tree branches overhead. She fell silent, though she was certain that the hawk could hear the loud poundings of her heart. After a while they hiked again through the bleached trees, until dusk fell and the wood turned dark. Dinah felt as though she were wandering through a gathering of ghosts. The Spade stopped abruptly and pushed his ear against the ground. After listening for a few seconds, he hopped to his feet.

"We'll camp here for the night." He bound his mare, Cyndy, to a tree and looked at Dinah to see if she would do the same.

She laughed at the idea. "Try to tie him there. You won't live long, but all the more reason to try." Morte collapsed in a moss pile a few feet away and began eating all the wild grasses within his reach. The Spade was gathering sticks into a pile. Dinah realized too late what he was doing. She dashed dirt toward the pile with her foot. "Stop! Don't build a fire, they'll see it!"

The Spade laughed as he produced a tiny muslin bag. "Ever see nightpowder?" Dinah shook her head. The Spade lit the fire with a flint, but as soon as he saw the first sign of a flicker, he dropped a pinch of the powder onto the growing flame. "Aye, the trick is to get it on when it's just a tiny thing. It won't work on a raging fire, or even a burning log."

Dinah watched in amazement as the flame grew—only instead of glowing with an orange heat, it was black, and emitted a clear smoke that disappeared into the sky. The flames still burned hot, and Dinah enjoyed the first feel of heat she'd felt on her face in a long time. The Spade roasted two rabbits he had speared that day and generously gave Dinah a whole one. She dived into it, relishing the drip of grease on her face. She threw the rest of her rabbit over to Morte, who cracked the bones between his teeth.

The Spade watched with disgust. "Unnatural, that is."

Dinah shrugged. When the Spade finished eating, he dropped the smallest portion of nightpowder into his pipe and leaned back against a rock. His ease infuriated her, and Dinah could contain herself no longer. "Tell me about Wardley."

The Spade inhaled a deep mouthful of his pipe and cleared his throat.

"So yeh want to know of the boy yeh left behind?"

Dinah thought long and hard before asking her question. "I would like to know any and all information that pertains to Wardley Ghane and the reasons behind any harms or dangers he might have encountered."

The Spade's drawn face scowled. "That seems like more than one question."

Dinah grinned wickedly. "I think it seems like a perfectly

valid question. After all, I'm just asking about Wardley."

"Yer asking a bit more, and I believe yeh know that."

"I believe that is what you believe." Dinah continued smiling. She watched his features change through the flickering onyx flame. Dinah didn't know much about the Spades—of all the Cards, they were the ones most shrouded in secrecy—but she did know that Spades loved to tell a good tale with their comrades, bloody tales of wars fought, of limbs lost, and of battle fever, tales that would make any other Wonderlander squirm. Dinah was baiting him—she could tell by the way his mouth twitched and the grinding of his filthy teeth. Sir Gorrann longed to tell her everything.

The Spade stood up in the clear night, the black flames of the fire kissing the tips of his boots. A thin trail of smoke curled out of the side of his mouth, and he began. "Well, if yeh must know, Wardley Ghane is alive." Dinah felt a sweet wave of relief wash over her, sweeter than anything she had ever tasted. A sob escaped her throat.

Sir Gorrann watched her closely. "On the day you fled—Wonderlanders now call it the 'Morning of Sorrows'—all the Cards were woken by their commanders in the early morning with the surprising news that the princess had murdered her own brother, his servants, and Heart Cards in cold blood."

Two lies and a single truth, Dinah thought. *I did kill two Heart Cards. I lanced one through the heart from behind, like a coward, and the other I pierced through the chest. Wardley killed yet another one in the stables to protect me.* The blood on her hands was growing thicker.

The Spade continued, ignorant to her whirling guilt. "As the sun rose outside, we were instructed to put on our armor and march out to meet the princess in front of the gates and to capture her—eh, you—dead or alive. Our commander, the great Spade Starey Belft, made it clear to us that dead was completely acceptable, due to the nature of yer crimes." The Spade cleared his throat. "I knew it to be a lie. The scar on my cheek confirmed it. The passion with which yeh had defended that silly wooden toy for yer brother had shown me that yeh could never do such a thing. Yer brother was never a threat to yer crown—it was yers for the taking, or so I thought. No, the only person who stood to gain from yer brother's murder was yer father. This all raced through my head, yeh see, as I strapped on my armor and headed out to secure the gates. We waited. The Cards returned and began to sniff around the stables. Then I saw yeh, a terrifying vision if there ever was one."

Dinah tilted her head, confused. The nightfire reflected off the Spade's face, making his eyes glimmer like coins in the darkness. "How so?"

"I saw yeh, Yer Highness, straddled across that massive black steed of yours, tearing out of the stable labyrinth like the devil himself was chasing yeh, a sword in yer hand, the cloak trailing behind yeh. I watched in awe as yeh plowed over helpless men without blinking, bent on revenge. I couldn't begin to fathom what yeh were doing, but yeh looked fierce as a dragon. As yeh were sprinting to the gate, the other two Hornhooves came out behind you, killing and maiming any man they came across. Do you know they killed ten men?"

More blood, thought Dinah, *more death because of me*. The Spade gave a light laugh. It bounced off the rocky land around them.

"Wonderlanders are still talking about it—they are calling you the 'Rebel Queen.'"

"But I'm not the Rebel Queen. That's not me," blurted Dinah. "I was terrified. I was fleeing for my life. I didn't even fully understand what was happening. Wardley put me on Morte and sent him running for the gates."

"Yes, but the townspeople don't know that. They only know what the king tells them, and that's very little. Because of the Morning of Sorrows, they *hate* yeh, but more important, they *fear* yeh. To everyone in the kingdom, it seemed like an attack, a last vengeance on Wonderland after killing your brother—a wild act, filled with fury. They believe yeh wanted to kill as many Heart Cards as you could before deserting the castle and leaving yer father to mourn his only son."

"That isn't true. I would never . . ." *But you would,* said a voice inside her. *You did kill innocent Cards. You can and you have.* The Spade threw another bunch of branches onto the black flames of the fire, which leaped even higher, their invisible smoke irritating Dinah's eyes. He continued.

"Trust me, it will be to yer advantage in the future."

The future? Dinah pushed herself off the rotted log she was perched on, her tone dripping with annoyance. "I don't understand what this has to do with Wardley. Tell me about Wardley."

"Ah, sorry. I'm getting there, Yer Highness. Because everything that happened to your stable boy—"

"*Wardley*," snapped Dinah. "His name is Wardley."

"Everything was a result of your actions that day, you tearing out of the castle like a mad bear let loose. I stayed there long enough to see yer father and his small cavalry pass through the gates in pursuit of yeh, and I'm not sure I've ever seen a man so bent on the destruction of another. He longs for his vengeance, and he will never stop thirsting for it."

In the past this statement would have sent Dinah into a flurry of tears, but now it just roused the boiling rage within her. She did not mourn the loss of her father anymore. He had taken everything from her. *I should have killed him in the forest last night*, she thought. *I had my chance for revenge and walked away from it.*

"When the King of Hearts returned from chasing you out of the castle, he was blinded with anger. He had lost the chase, and everyone in Wonderland knew it, especially the Cards. He maimed three fruit sellers just because they didn't get out of his way fast enough, and there were a handful of townspeople that he beat so savagely yeh can hardly recognize them. He also finished off one of the white Hornhooves, only because she wasn't able to catch up with yeh." The Spade ran his fingers across his knife belt as he stood, and Dinah suddenly felt a bit unsafe as the anger in his tone rose.

"Wardley," she whispered.

"Er, right. I know a Heart Card who stands guard at the palace infirmary. He says that after the king killed the Hornhoov, he barged into the wing where they were treating yer stable boy and demanded his blood as well. He was crazed, knocking over carts and beds. The doctor on duty argued that Wardley's blood had already been paid and that he had a very real stab wound to prove his innocence. The king pushed past him, his sword in hand . . ." Dinah felt like she might faint under the bright stars shining that night, spiraled above in a glowing, circular pattern. "By some miracle, the king refrained once he saw that the blood flowing over the table and onto the floor all belonged to Wardley. He was unconscious, his wound raw and deep." Dinah winced, remembering the feeling of her sword separating his muscle, ringing against the bone, the pained face of the boy she loved.

"He had been found slumped over in the stables. Wardley's story was that he had slipped away from the Heart Cards when they were entering the castle to try to stop yeh, making his way to the stables. The next thing he knew, there was a bloody gaping hole in his arm and a huge lump on his head."

Dinah said a silent prayer of thanks that Wardley was so smart, so clever. Even in the Black Towers he had been astute and quick on his feet.

"The king wanted his head nonetheless, but was convinced otherwise by his council—Cheshire most likely, crafty snake that he is. The execution of such a handsome young Card, one who was so well liked and potentially the next Knave of Hearts, would surely be frowned upon by the court and the kingdom. In the end, it was a political move." The Spade shook his head with a cavernous laugh.

"Of course, his reputation for being one of the most-skilled fighters in the Cards has since disappeared, and now he is known for being bested by the princess. He is called 'Wardley the Weak,' though always behind his back, as a wise man would not say it when he holds a sword in his hand. He still bears the Card clasp, but he mostly works on rebuilding the stables yeh so recklessly tore down."

Dinah tried to manage her breathing, but the sob she had been holding in broke forth from her lips, and she buried her face in her hands. Wardley, once the brightest star in Wonderland, the future Knave of Hearts, would be mocked for the rest of his life, all because he had saved hers. Her body shook with sobs before the Spade, who looked alarmed at her sudden rush of emotion.

Dinah was embarrassed. "I'm sorry. It was my fault. . . . Wardley . . . he saved me. He put me on Morte and unlocked the stable gates. He gave me his sword and told me to stab him. I would have lain down and waited for the king if it wasn't for him." She wiped her nose on the corner of her sleeve.

The Spade's lips turned up in a half smile. "You'd surely be dead if you'd have done that. I doubt your father has room for two girls on the throne."

Dinah jerked her head up. "Vittiore?"

"You must have fathomed that she would take yer place."

Yes, Dinah had imagined it, but it was always a waking nightmare, her worst fear come true. Vittiore, walking up the aisle of the Great Hall as her court bowed before her. Vittiore, her long golden curls pressed down as the beautiful twisting crown that Charles had made was lowered onto her head. In her mind, she saw Vittiore, sitting in the Heart throne next to her father, ruling Wonderland when she was nothing better than a piece of rotten fruit from the mountain villages. Dinah let out a blunt, angry cry and kicked the rotting log below her into the fire. *My father has taken everything.*

"That whore will never truly be the queen. She is a pawn in my father's game, a tool that he used to push me out. She knew that my brother would be murdered and did nothing."

Dinah saw the flicker of a smile pass over the Spade's dark features. "Indeed. But she is beloved by the people. They are grateful that she survived the Rebel Queen's rampage. The talk among the common people is that you tried to murder sweet Vittiore but couldn't get into her room."

"That is a *lie*," whispered Dinah intensely. "I was never anywhere near her room that night. I only went to Charles's room, where I saw my brother . . ." Her voice collapsed, a mix of anger and grief. "I saw his broken body lying on a slab of stone. His eyes looked at nothing."

The Spade was silent, and for a few minutes there was only the crackle of nightfire.

Finally, the Spade spoke. "There's nothing to be done now. 'Tis still the early days of these changes. Vittiore is queen and sits beside your father. There is unrest in Wonderland because the king used the increase in the number of Cards and weapons to justify raising taxes. Many people in the kingdom are starving as he reinforces the Cards. When we left, turrets were being built around the perimeter of the iron walls."

Dinah wiped her tears away and worked at keeping her voice steady. "The Iron Gates? Did we break them?" She vaguely remembered the sides of the gates clipping Morte's shoulder before they were thrust open. The Spade laughed.

"Well, the king doesn't feel that the Iron Gates were enough to keep his traitorous daughter in, so he is strengthening them to make sure they keep her and everyone else out."

Dinah gave a wry laugh. "To keep me out? What an idea. I have no intention of ever going back there. I'll be killed the moment I appear in Wonderland proper! I will never see the palace again." *Or Harris. Or the beautiful stained-glass heart that sits outside my mother's room, the one that shades the world in red.*

The Spade took a last inhale of his pipe before dumping its contents into the fire. "Perhaps. But I think the king fears more than just the return of the princess."

"The Yurkei?"

"This is the end of your answers for tonight."

"There is nothing more to tell me of Wardley?"

"No. His shoulder's still healing. He spends his days

in the stables, wiping the dung off his face that is thrown at him by orphans."

But he is alive, thought Dinah. *His heart beats.*

She had begun to ask of his family when the Spade turned slightly, his ears pointed at the sky. *"Be silent!"* he whispered. Dinah froze in place. Without making a sound, the Spade ran over to his pack and withdrew a bow and arrow. Her heart thudded in her ears, and she looked at the dark wood around them as a shiver of dread made its way up her spine. She took in the moss-covered rocks and the thin white trees that ringed their nightfire. *There are worse places to be laid to rest*, she thought. *At least I'm here under the stars.*

The Spade lifted the bow, his muscled arms quivering as he tracked something across the dark sky that Dinah couldn't see. Finally, he exhaled and released the arrow. Dinah heard a *thwap*, followed by the sound of something falling through dried leaves. The Spade darted into the wood. She was alone. *The day I find out what he wants*, she told herself, *is the day I will leave this Spade behind.* There was a rustling from the trees, and something landed with a sickening crack at her feet. It was the hawk, the tracking hawk, its beautiful deep red feathers mottled with black blood, an arrow through its neck. Dinah looked up at the Spade—and the admiration written across her face betrayed her.

He gave a laugh at her surprise. "Chicken, Princess?"

Five

For the first time in weeks, Dinah slept long and deep, without dreams of bloody Heart Cards or anything else that woke her in terror. It was late morning when she rose to a loud clanging. She shielded her eyes as she sat up. The Spade was clanging his swords together and watching how the blades ran over each other. Dinah was understandably unnerved by this.

"Morning, Princess." The Spade tossed a small loaf of bread in her direction, and Dinah tore into it with ravenous bites. "Not very delicate, are yeh?"

She made a face in his direction.

"Now, get yerself up so I can begin yer training. I've seen eight-year-old girls that can wield a sword better than yeh."

"I highly doubt that," replied Dinah, brushing the crumbs off her cheeks. She handed a small piece of her bread to Morte, who almost bit her fingers off.

"On the contrary, I was raised in a village where every child could defend themselves."

Dinah was curious about this man. "Where was your village? And what makes you think your children could defend themselves? Spades can't even have chil—"

She didn't have a chance to finish. The Spade swept both her feet out from under her, and Dinah landed hard on the small of her back. All the air rushed from her lungs. She barely had time to react before the tip of his sword drew a line across her cheek. He bowed before her. "Now we have matching scars."

Dinah leaped up and flung herself against him, and they both tumbled to the ground. The Spade easily flipped her facedown into the dirt and then proceeded to keep her down with his boot, standing on top of her. Though his actions were quick and rough, his tone remained calm. "Yeh'll not say one word about my family, understand? Now, are yeh ready to learn?"

Dinah writhed under his foot before shouting at him, "Get off me. I command it!"

The Spade's gruff laugh echoed off the rock faces around them as he continued to balance on top of her. "Ah, Princess. Before yeh can learn to fight, yeh must let go of the idea that anyone in Wonderland gives a care about yer fate. Yer no longer a royal playing sticks with the stable boy. Yer no longer a princess—or anyone, for that matter. Yer a wretch, a wanderer in the forest. Think about it. Are yeh her? Are yeh that girl, the girl who would be queen?"

Dinah considered for a moment, her face bleeding into the dirt. He was right. She was no longer the princess who loved to watch pink snowflakes swirling down from the cloudy sky, one who could command the bowed knee of every person in the room. She was here, in the middle of the wilderness. She was starving, she was broken and bleeding, and there was a Spade literally standing on her back. All this and yet Dinah felt more in control of her fate than she had the past few months at the palace. There was a freedom in having nothing to lose.

"Let me stand. I said, let me stand!" She rolled over quickly, which caused him to lose his balance. Then she grabbed hold of the Spade's leg and dug her teeth into his calf.

He let out a yell and hopped away. "Yeh bit me! Who bites someone?"

Dinah shuffled to her feet, unsteady, bleeding from the lip and covered with dirt. She spat on the ground. "C'mon, you dirty Spade—teach me to fight."

He rubbed his beard. "Ah, there's the girl who slapped me for a toy, I knew yeh were there somewhere." He tossed Wardley's sword at her, and Dinah managed to catch it without slicing her hand open. This, however, was to be the highlight of her day. The rest of that morning was spent getting bruised, hit, and cut open by the blunt end of Sir

Gorrann's sword. Every strike was deflected and every move of her body was analyzed in an effort to find her weaknesses, which turned out to be *everything*.

As he flew around her, his voice never stopped lecturing. "Any move off balance and yeh belong to the enemy. A good swordsman can tell when his opponent is off balance and will use it to his advantage."

Dinah tried to maintain perfect balance while wielding the sword but it never worked—she was always tipped slightly to one side or the other. The Spade continued to knock her to the ground with ease, but after a few times she leaped up quickly, at the ready to fight again.

"That was good. Work on getting back in the fight. Yeh must learn to respond quickly when yer down. It can make the difference between victory and defeat. Now, give me back yer sword. We'll try again tomorrow to correct yer balance, but until then yeh do not deserve it."

Dinah clutched Wardley's blade close to her chest. *I have earned the right to this blade*, she thought, *I will not give it up so easily.* She felt bold. "Come and take it!" she declared.

He did, and left her lying on a rocky ledge, out of breath, with a bloody nose.

Once the morning ended, Sir Gorrann erased all traces of them at the campsite and they continued to weave their way deeper into the Yurkei Mountains. The terrain was ever changing. The ground rose and fell in rocky slopes, like waves of rock that crested and broke, spilling their huge boulders upon gorgeous green valleys before rising again. It was a physically exhausting climb, and Dinah periodically looked longingly at Morte, but he ignored her completely. Only once, when Dinah slipped on a rock and tore her shin open from top to bottom did Morte pause and lift his leg. Dinah wearily climbed onto his massive back while Sir Gorrann watched with fascination.

"Thank you," she breathed to him, letting her hand run over his smooth neck before he nipped at her. He climbed easily through the jagged peaks that were increasingly a struggle for Sir Gorrann's brown mare, Cyndy. The air became thinner and cleaner, and Dinah relished the sharp, cold breaths that cleared her mind.

They stopped to camp for the night, and Dinah was allowed her one question as the Spade stoked his night-fire. She asked about Harris, and learned that he had been imprisoned in the Black Towers. He was part of a group being forced into slave labor, helping to reinforce the Iron Gates, and so Sir Gorrann said that Harris was outside for a few hours most days. He confessed that the old man looked broken, weary, and sad. He was often covered with bruises and cuts inflicted by the Clubs. This news broke Dinah's heart, and afterward there wasn't a day that she didn't think of Harris's kind face and soft hands. He had delivered her from her mother's womb, loved her the way her father should have, taught her everything she knew, and now he was in pain. It was unforgivable, and the white-hot rage she felt toward her father could have burned the Twisted Wood to the ground. To her devastation, she learned that Emily had been beheaded for treason in a public execution, based on the shabby testimony of Nanda and Palma, Vittiore's ladies-in-waiting. The Spade didn't talk to her for the rest of that evening, and Dinah was grateful. She stared out at the

Wonderland stars, bunched together in small clusters, and didn't bother to wipe the tears that dripped down her face. Her life was like nightfire—a place that once burned with bright hope, now nothing more than a flickering blackness, her suffering invisible to the naked eye.

In the weeks that followed, she woke sore but rested. Together, they gulped down a quick breakfast of stale bread and game before her training began. After days of working on balance, Dinah finally got her sword back, and with it her pride. She was covered in bruises, but each one had taught her a painful lesson, one that she would not soon forget. Pain cemented things in the brain the way reading did not.

After sparring, they continued to make their way east, going painfully slowly as they navigated their way over pebbly ground and fields of strewn boulders. The Yurkei

Mountains were upon them now, and the farther they got from the Twisted Wood, the less she feared her father finding them. The rocky outcroppings and grooves in the earth provided minimal protection once they reached the tree line, but there was no one around. The Spade had delivered them from the king's hands, as promised.

In the evenings, Sir Gorrann would tell her of the politics and rumors swirling around Wonderland. Some she knew and some she did not know. He told her dark stories of the Spades, stories that entertained while making her blood curdle. He never spoke of his own past, which made Dinah even more curious about where he had come from and why he was here. When she pressed him for answers, he simply walked away, leaving her in uncomfortable silence.

After one morning's lesson—which consisted of repeatedly striking targets that Sir Gorrann had marked with charred wood—they started their hike early due to the abundance of ominous clouds in the west, and continued to make their way toward the mountains. The weather had turned in the last few days. Cheerful and glossy spring had changed into sopping warm rains and foggy nights. As she was almost constantly damp, drenched, or drying, Dinah had never known that being wet could be so miserable.

The pair circled their way around boulders that resembled hulking granite giants, ones that even seemed to dwarf Morte. That day had proved the most challenging climb so far, and both were exhausted from leading their steeds over the rocky switchbacks that led up a nearly sheer cliff face. Dinah felt a question alight on her tongue. The Spade had shared so little about himself, and her curiosity grew more potent every day.

Hoping that the discomfort and distraction of the climb would ease his fury, Dinah dared to speak the question: "Sir Gorrann, what happened to your family?"

The Spade flinched as he nicked his arm on a sharp rock outcropping. "Damn! Look what yeh made me do. Been dying to ask, have yeh?"

Dinah shrugged, the motion giving Morte's new leather reins a shake, a gift from the Spade. Morte regarded them humorously, seeing how he could break them on a moment's notice. Most of the day, they were rarely anything other than decorative.

"Perhaps. It's either that or tell me exactly where we're going in the Yurkei Mountains."

The Spade took a deep breath and stared aimlessly at the sky with his dark gold eyes. "Fine. I'll tell yeh about my family. What I'm about to share cannot be repeated, understand? And once I tell it, yeh may not ask any questions about it. I'll not have you pestering me for feelings that I've long buried."

Dinah nodded. "I won't. Promise."

"Fine, then." He turned slightly back to look at her, his long gray hair blowing in the breeze. "Cling to the wall, Princess, or this coming wind will rip yeh right off."

Dinah pressed herself against the stony slate and continued to watch him silently. The Spade stared off into the distance, his eyes focused on something she couldn't see.

"I grew up in the Twisted Wood, farther north from where we've been. That's why I have a bit of an accent, yeh see? A small village called Dianquill. Yeh've probably never heard of it." Dinah shook her head, her eyes trained on the hundred foot drop before her.

"I was just fifteen years old when I met Amabel. I saw

her out of the corner of my eye, this tiny red-haired girl, obviously hungry and dressed in filthy rags. I gave her some Julla fruit that I had in my bag, and she scampered off into the trees. 'Twas weeks later when she found me out hunting. In return for food, she taught me how to track. Though I might seem skilled to yeh now, I am nothing compared to Amabel. She could track a deer for a hundred miles and at the same time follow the path of a man who had walked that land twenty days prior."

Sir Gorrann paused to take a long drink from his waterskin. "We married when I was nineteen, and I tell yeh, I have never loved another woman. Every morning when my eyes open, I can see her face—her long red hair, her bright eyes, wild as the sea. Hunting became almost too easy with Amabel's tracking skills. We had a bounty, and life was sweet and easy. After our third year of marriage, we welcomed a daughter, Ioney. She looked like her mother. I bet Amabel that I could never love anything more than her, but I lost that wager the moment I first laid eyes on our little Ioney. Our family was complete, and I wanted for nothing. I was a happy young man. Then *they* came. It was a damp spring day, not unlike this one . . ."

His voice sputtered out. The Spade had stopped moving, and Dinah held her position on the rock. Tears were gathering in his eyes, and she saw his weathered hands clenching with emotion. Though she was utterly fascinated, winding tendrils of guilt began to snake through her for asking him to recount these details. "You don't have to . . ."

"*Quiet, girl!*" he snapped. "Yeh asked, and yeh'll hear it. It's been a spell since I've spoken of them." His mouth distorted with pain as he continued his story.

"As I was saying, it was spring, and the warm rains had come and gone. I was out hunting a white bear, the same kind you told me almost took yer limbs, when I saw smoke rising from the village. I ran back, but it was too late. The entire village was smoldering; no building was left untouched. Several of my friends had been slaughtered defending their homes. Most of the women and children had been left alive, but the majority of the men had been cut to pieces. My father was hanging from a burning log that had once been my childhood home. All the villagers' food and livestock had been taken, their homes gone forever. An entire village, wiped out in less than an hour by a few cruel Cards."

Dinah's eyes narrowed. "Cards? From Wonderland Palace? Not the Yurkei?"

"I thought it was the Yurkei at first as well, but no. A friend who was dying in my arms told me that while some of the riders had been painted to look like Yurkei, they were undoubtedly Cards. The arrow buried in his stomach was topped with a red glass heart, so there was little doubt. Indeed, it had been Heart Cards, on their way to fight with Yurkei. Their provisions had run low, so they had taken what they wanted from my village. I gave my friend a quick end and climbed upon my horse and galloped for my home, faster than I had ever ridden in my life."

Dinah longed to stop his story, to put her hands over his mouth to save her the horror of what was coming.

A tear made its way down his face. "I was too late for my darling girls. The Cards had come across Amabel while she was tending our herb garden. She lay motionless on the ground, her red hair wet with the blood that flowed from her chest, my brave love. Her hand clutched a bow and arrow, and I can only imagine that she intended to use it to defend our child. For this she had been shot clean through the heart. I longed to hold her there forever, her body still warm, but I had to find my daughter."

Dinah closed her eyes and pressed against the cool rock face, desperate to hear no more.

"Ioney was inside the house, although there wasn't a house anymore, just a charred pile of smoking wood and fallen timber. There was only bones left of my little girl, my Ioney."

Her eyes blurring with tears, Dinah looked away from Sir Gorrann, out into the open air before them, a vast view of honey-colored valleys and gray rock. Up until now, she had mistakenly believed that she was the only one who had suffered, the only one who had reason to grieve. Her childishness convicted her and she felt her face flush with shame.

The Spade continued. "Feeling sad that yeh asked, are yeh? 'Twas a dark night with dark thoughts when I lay beside my love. The next day, I buried Amabel and Ioney under their favorite berry bush in the woods, an unmarked grave. I planted Amabel's treasured orchids in a circle around their grave, sang them their favorite song and departed with my horse as evening fell. I took nothing with me aside from some food, a blanket, and every weapon I could find."

A vengeful smile played over his face, and Dinah feared she might be sick. "I rode my horse so hard he died after two days. I left him in the woods, barely stopping to put him out of his misery. From there, I tracked the Cards to the edge of the Yurkei Mountains, where they were attempting to find their way into Hu-Yuhar, the hidden Yurkei city, and failing miserably. It was a small group of only six men."

Sir Gorrann smiled and stroked his beard with disturbing fondness. Dinah was suddenly very afraid of him.

"I stalked and killed one each night, so that the rest might live in fear before their death's imminent arrival. They called me the Night Ghost and wrongly assumed that I was a Yurkei assassin. When at last my vengeance was complete, I left their bodies in the Twisted Wood, just like they had left my Amabel to die. I lived for months in these hills, eventually finding the will to continue on living. I made my way to Wonderland proper. There was nothing left for me in the Twisted Wood. I never wanted to see those places again, those places in my memory where I had first seen my wife, or where we had conceived our child."

Sir Gorrann cleared his throat and blinked before continuing along the uphill trail. His voice steadied. "I made my way to the palace, where I was blindsided by its size and wealth. I fell in with unsavory bedfellows, and soon was stealing to eat, then stealing to live. I was a good thief when I wasn't drinking, but unfortunately that was more often than not. I was caught breaking into a lady of the court's house while attempting to steal her jewels, so drunk I could barely stand. Her husband was a beast of a man and rightly beat me to a bloody pulp. I was thrown into the Black Towers." Dinah's mouth fell open, and he managed to give her a rough smile.

"Yes, Princess, yeh aren't the only one who has seen the horrors of the Black Towers. Luckily for me I was in the Thieves' Tower. I was never strapped against its terrible roots." Dinah said a silent prayer that Harris was not being strapped to the tree. Seeing him devoured from the inside as Faina Baker had been would surely be enough to break her.

"I was imprisoned in the Black Towers for two years. It was a dark time, but I managed to befriend a young Club who told me everything he knew about Wonderland, the

Black Towers, and the Cards. I was forced to join the Spades, for which I am ever grateful. Thanks to the Spades, I had food, a place to live, and a purpose. Eventually I became the lead tracker for the king, and that led me to being here with yeh now."

Dinah frowned as she sent a scattering of pebbles rolling down the steep mountainside. "I still don't understand why you sought to help me. You're a Spade. Therefore you are loyal to the king and the Cards. You have betrayed your oaths in a grand way."

The Spade climbed up onto an overhead ledge to view their surroundings and then looked down on Dinah, who observed him with confused admiration. Leading Morte, she scrambled up the path behind him, finally approaching the summit of the mountain.

The Spade stood before her, his stare intense. "Indeed. I have broken my vows by helping yeh. Surely yeh've assumed that there was something I left out of the story. One man remains, just one left, and my vengeance against him will be a prize above rubies. A young man, a young king, recently crowned by his father, who ordered the raid on my village, was present for the murder of my family before he was called back to Wonderland on royal business. This man I could not kill silently while creeping through the woods, for he was guarded night and day by fighters more skilled than I. To take his life is not enough. I must see him fall, to see everything that he loves stripped from him, which as far as I can see, is only power."

Dinah stared at the Spade as fat drops of rain drenched them both. Lightning snaked across the gray sky. "Vengeance. This is why I help yeh, and this is why we hike endlessly through these mountains. So that someday we will both have justice for the loved ones taken from us."

Dinah stared at the Spade, not sure what to say while her head reeled with potent thoughts and emotions. An empty hiss of air escaped her lips as she wiped a stray tear from her eye with the back of her hand, mingling with the rain that was now coming in sideways. Her pain was nothing compared to his loss, and yet she felt a sting of anger burning through her. His motivations had finally shown, and she was aware of just how close she was to a man who could have taken her life a dozen times before she woke.

Finally, she found the words she was looking for and began to speak. "Sir Gorrann, I am sorry for the loss of your family, but I have no intention of returning to Wonderland Palace. Not tomorrow, not ever. Now, if you will please tell me where you are leading me, I'm certain we can—"

"*Be silent!*" hissed the Spade, his head turning swiftly to the west. Morte's ears perked up. There was only silence, and then the crunch of a leaf, the sound of a step on the trail below them. "Hurry!" he whispered. "Someone's following us. We must pass over this summit, and quickly."

Fear churned through Dinah as she gripped the leather reins, urging Morte as quickly as she dared up and over the rocky slope. Coming over the rocks, the pair ran into a sheer cliff face. An enormous slab of gray rock loomed before them, extending its jagged ends into the noon sun. Hundreds of boulders filled the small space, as if a giant had been playing with his toys and left them in a terrible pile.

"We're trapped!" Dinah snapped. "Where did you lead us?"

Sir Gorrann was scanning the face of the wall, searching for something Dinah couldn't see. There were several footsteps now, echoing off the ledges below, the sound of more than a dozen men inching ever closer. At first Dinah was confused as to why they had not been swarmed over already, but then she understood. Whoever tracked them wanted to push them over the cliff face. Sir Gorrann continued to search between boulders.

"What are you doing?" Dinah screamed. "We have to fight!" Finally, Sir Gorrann found what he was looking for. Two boulders, perfectly aligned, of equal shape and size. Upon first glance, there was nothing extraordinary about them, but on further inspection, their identical shape, marking, and color was unnerving. Dinah ran to Sir Gorrann, her sword drawn.

"Put that away," he mumbled. "You could not fight what threatens to push us off this ledge." As they crept around the boulders, the Spade took a surprising step between them. Dinah blinked several times before she was able to decipher the illusion. What she thought were two boulders was actually one carved to look like two separate shapes. Inside a narrow space between the two rounded forms hid a tall hole, almost impossible to spot unless you were standing at the perfect angle. Dinah knew she never would have been able to find it on her own.

"Through here!" shouted the Spade. Something churned in her stomach as she looked into the inky tunnel. It was a lurking, terrible feeling, a fear that distorted and confused. She recognized it immediately—this was how she felt when the root had twisted into her mouth. There was evil in that tunnel.

"No, I can't go in there."

Sir Gorrann grabbed her arm and practically dragged her inside. "We have no choice, Princess. Move!"

She opened her mouth to object, but there were no other options. Head bowed, she followed Sir Gorrann's mare through the narrow opening. Morte gave a great huff and stomped the ground furiously, his hooves sending booming echoes through the quarry. The ground seemed to shudder. Finally, once Dinah took her hands off his reins, he ducked his head and entered the tunnel willingly. His flanks brushed against the wall. He was unfamiliar and uncomfortable in this rocky terrain. His ears were flattened against his head, and Dinah could see his muscles tensed and ready to run.

She felt a sudden rush of panic.

Sir Gorrann, his mare, Dinah, and Morte were stacked end to end, moving as quickly as they dared. If Morte should panic and bolt, they would all be trampled under his crushing weight. Sir Gorrann glanced back at Morte, his face pale and drawn. He had obviously come to the same conclusion. They paused, their hearts humming loudly in their closely drawn quarters.

"This is a wicked place," breathed Sir Gorrann. "Let's hurry. Keep yer devil calm." The tunnel was maybe a half mile long, and from the moment they entered, an all-encompassing darkness draped them like a heavy blanket. Overhead, Dinah could hear the slight slithering of roots, a whispered hiss, and the sound of a thousand tiny legs. A liquid dripped onto her cheek, warm and smelling of blood. Her hand brushed up against something wet and rubbery and she leaped toward the mare with a shriek. Morte was becoming more agitated, and Dinah forced herself to remain calm as a wet tendril caressed her cheek in the darkness. Something was crawling in her hair that made tiny clicking sounds with a sharp mouth. It scuttled across her forehead and leaped onto the wall. The walls around them were alive, raising their voices in a hissed chorus. *Evil, evil, evil.* Sir Gorrann pressed himself against the wall to let Cyndy pass, and Dinah felt his hand close around her wrist, grateful for the warmth of his calloused fingers. A creature wet and long encircled their wrists before slithering away into the tunnel.

"Do not run. Do not run." He repeated the mantra again and again, convincing himself rather than Dinah. Dinah did not need the reminder. As terrible as the tunnel was—and it was the foulest place she could ever dream of, a place of nightmares—there would be nothing worse than being trampled alive and left to die in this place, to have your body consumed slowly by whatever demons thrived in this dark corridor. Her pace stayed steady, and her hand tightened around Sir Gorrann's in a show of strength. She would keep him calm. They stayed silent, afraid their voices would collapse the rock inward, or even worse, stir up the invisible creatures to aggression. A wild fear of the unknown pressed against Dinah's brain and she found herself remembering every dark thing that had ever happened to her. She saw death, bodies, the king. Charles, with worms crawling out of his eyes. Vittiore, wearing the crown her brother made her. The dead farmer, the arrow in his back leaking blood.

She stumbled once, twice. Sir Gorrann was having a hard time as well, murmuring violent things to himself as he bumped off the wall, falling over his own feet. Some slithery heavy thing had settled on his shoulder, and he struggled to wrench it away. Dinah kept walking. She couldn't help him. Her hope was gone. The steam from Morte's nostrils was burning her elbow now, his muzzle pressed against her back. He was pushing faster now. *We're going to die in here,* she thought. Another thought occurred to her—perhaps they were already dead. Perhaps this tunnel *was* death, in all its hideous finality.

She couldn't remember who she was. How did she get here again? A creature was prying at her mouth. *Might as well open it,* she thought. *What could be the harm?* Then warm light appeared at the end of the tunnel, a hazy pinkish spot, welcoming and safe. It throbbed through the darkness. Cyndy broke into a sprint toward it and Sir Gorrann followed, forgetting all previous instruction, so desperate to be free from this underground hell. Slimy, terrible things detached themselves from Dinah's hair and wrists, slithering down her legs and back into the darkness. The light blazed through the dark. She burst through into its glorious pinkness and fell to her knees beside Sir Gorrann. He pushed her out of the way just before Morte's gigantic body collapsed in a heap right where she had been kneeling.

They lay on the ground, gasping, taking in heavy breaths of delicious, sweet air, so happy to be free of the tunnel. Minutes passed. There was nothing sweeter than being alive. Morte whinnied happily beside her, rolling on the soft carpet of flowers to erase the stench of the tunnel. When she finally felt balanced again, Dinah peered down at her hands on the ground. Purple flowers, the same color that Cheshire wore so often, opened and shut before her eyes, their blooms radiating individual rays of soft light. With each pulse of the petal, a tiny tendril of red lashed out, a pink light on the tip of the stamen. It was remarkable and strange all at once, and her eyes followed the ground until she saw that one flower led to a patch of flowers, and the patch of flowers led to a field. They were in an entire valley full of blinking purple and pink flowers, pouring out light and—she held her hand over the tip of the flower—*Yes, heat.*

The flowers radiated a warm heat when they popped open, which accounted for the heavenly air that flowed through this field. The grass was a bright green, and felt more like a soft pillow than a wooded forest floor. Dinah felt the overwhelming desire to slip off her boots and run laughing through the flowers. It could only be called a hysterical happiness. She was drunk with it.

"My gods," she heard Sir Gorrann mutter, and Dinah stood up. The Spade rested his hand on her arm and with a gentle touch tilted her head upward. They both looked in wonder. Thousands of enormous, swirly mushrooms filled the field. They were huge, as tall as trees in most places. Their stems were wider than Dinah, trunk-like white stalks that led up into a thick, billowy explosion of color, the horizon like a bucket of parasols. They exploded from the ground, each unique in its varied colors and type, giving the overall effect of being in a hazy dream. Dinah turned in a circle. The valley was deep and long, a maze of color and fantastic curling shapes, each mushroom standing proudly against the sky.

Dinah blinked. She suddenly wasn't sure how long she had been staring at the mushrooms. Had she been here an hour or a minute? She looked over at Sir Gorrann. The Spade stood rooted in the same place he had been before, his mouth agape. Dinah began walking toward one of the mushrooms. Its cap was a brilliant yellow with swirls of glittering orange and red, like someone had taken a wet paintbrush to the top. Underneath the cap, a warm white light pulsed within its gills. They seemed to contract with each burst of light, as if they were breathing. The mushroom was utterly intoxicating, perhaps the most attractive thing she had ever seen. It seemed to be calling to her. Dinah reached out to touch the stem.

"Don't." The deep voice broke her trance and Dinah's hand jerked to a stop. The Spade walked up beside her. "Don't touch them. They might be poisonous. We don't know. On the other hand . . ."

"I want to eat them," whispered Dinah, her mouth watering at the thought.

Sir Gorrann scratched his beard, his hand trembling with want. "I do as well, which is exactly why I think we shouldn't. Let's continue on our way."

Dinah wanted to do anything but leave. Instead, she simply nodded. Her eyes took in every stem, every inch of the mushrooms. Together they walked silently through the field, the fungi stretching out in all directions, seemingly never ending. Dinah watched with fascination as they passed a pink-and-white-striped mushroom with a black stem and yellow gills, a bright blue mushroom the color and depth of the sky, and a deep purple mushroom with a stem covered in a thousand tiny mushrooms of the same color. The light in the valley faded into a soothing glow. It was something otherworldly, the most extraordinary thing Dinah had ever seen, the exact opposite of the dark tunnel from which they had emerged. Sir Gorrann didn't speak, but the Spade had drawn his sword for some reason that Dinah couldn't fully comprehend. Morte walked behind them, eating everything in sight. There was no way Dinah could stop him in this valley of rich food, and she watched him with envy as he gulped down a pure white mushroom that appeared to be made of frosting. Her steps fell silently on the soft lawn. Twisty tendrils curled up from the ground, as thick as a man's arm, as they passed. The curls gave a tiny shake when her foot landed beside them, as if they were stirring from a deep sleep.

I could stay here forever, thought Dinah. *I could lie underneath the mushrooms and simply watch their colors pulse with this . . . enthralling life.* Dinah let her eyes linger on a pink mushroom, its rich fuchsia the same color as the inside of a Julla fruit. Tiny glowing stars dotted its cap. "Oh," breathed Dinah, amazed at the beauty of it all. She reached for the mushroom. An odd cry echoed through the valley, such a strange sound in this peaceful haven of light and warmth. It sounded like a crane. The cry was followed by another, and then she heard a *whump*. She knew that sound. Her face distorted with terror as she spun around. The first arrow took the Spade off his feet. He flew backward onto the grass, a white-feathered arrow protruding from his chest. Two more arrows landed on either side of him. The valley grew lighter as all the mushrooms suddenly radiated with blinding white light. A second arrow landed just past her feet, another in front of her. She blinked in confusion.

Wake up! she screamed at herself. *You are under attack!* Her thoughts finally connected, and she blindly ran, arrows falling around her like rain. Dinah plunged through the mushrooms, ducking and bobbing as arrows whizzed past her face.

"Morte!" she screamed. "Morte!" Suddenly, he was upon her, his black hide rippling with excitement. He barely even stopped moving long enough for her to step onto his leg and vault herself onto the nape of his neck. They were flying, his muscles pounding like thunder beneath her, the rainbow light a colored blur that flashed past. Dinah watched with horror as a line of feathered warriors appeared before them. They were hundreds deep, each holding a notched arrow, each one trained on her and Morte. *The Yurkei.* Morte wheeled to the left, but they were there as well, and to the right, emerging from between the mushrooms like ghosts in the darkness. *Had they been there the whole time?* Morte whinnied and stepped backward. Something was wrong with him. He was stumbling, jumping, falling over his feet. The warriors slowly moved toward them. Dinah and Morte were surrounded on all sides.

Morte began to buck, and Dinah clutched his mane to keep from falling off. When he landed, she nudged him forward. If there was no passage leading away from the Yurkei, she would go through them. Morte would crush them under his mighty hooves, even if he was acting strangely. Dinah drew her sword.

"DINAH, STOP!" The voice plowed through the valley, strong and deep. The light from the mushrooms dimmed at the sound. She turned her head in surprise. It was the first time Sir Gorrann had ever said her name. He stood, looking very much alive, in the midst of a hundred Yurkei warriors, their arrows drawn, all pointing at Dinah and Morte. Blood leaked steadily from his shoulder, but there was no sign of a chest wound. *Armor*, she thought. *He still has his Spade armor on. Thank the gods.* The wild thudding of her heart shook her body as Morte wheeled and turned again.

Sir Gorrann raised his voice. "Dinah, do not fight! They will kill you with a hundred arrows before you cross their line. We are surrendering. Put down your sword." The Spade took his sword and laid it on the ground before raising his arms above his head. There was a murmuring in the crowd, and Dinah's eyes widened as the Yurkei parted. The mushrooms began to hum with light and sound. The warriors all extended their arms and pressed the base of their palms together, thumbs linked, fingers spread. Like wings. Dinah heard a familiar thudding, and her stomach clenched.

A tan Hornhoov emerged out of the dim light, and astride him, a fearsome-looking man. His hair was as white as milk, shaved back in a long strip that caressed his shoulder blades. Stripes of white paint covered his deeply tanned and muscular body, his radiant blue eyes visible even from a distance. On his head was a woven headdress of feathers, white and blue and gathered in a circle at the crown before cascading down his back. The rest of the Yurkei watched him with rapt attention, their hands still spread before themselves. He gave the slightest nod and their arms dropped back to their original position—aiming arrows at her and Morte. He was almost upon her now: Mundoo, the chief of the Yurkei.

A cold fear shot through her as she remembered all the terrible stories she had heard about this warrior chief. He raised his hand to her, his voice steady and calm. "Girl. You have trespassed into the sacred burial ground of the Yurkei tribe and will now be punished as such: you must give us your steed, your supplies, and all of your food and then you may go with your lives. Otherwise, you will be pierced through with the arrows of my strong warriors. They do not miss."

Dinah sat perfectly still, surprised at his perfect grasp of the Wonderland language. This seemed like a fair deal, but she did not want to part with Morte. Mundoo was eyeing him greedily—who knew what they would do to him.

Dinah coughed. "Jewels and gold are worth much more than this horse. I can get you all of those and more."

Mundoo gave a click of his tongue and his pale Horn-hoov approached, steam hissing aggressively out from his nose in Morte's direction. The mare was almost the same size as Morte, the color of the purest sand, her white mane braided through with blue ribbons and paint.

Mundoo narrowed his glowing blue eyes as he neared them. "But that is not just a steed, my lady, as you well know." As Mundoo grew closer, Dinah saw his blue eyes widen just before he drew his own arrow, pointed straight at her throat.

"Iy-Joyera! Iy-Joyera!" The tribe moved swiftly toward her, all arrows trained on Morte.

Mundoo stared past his quivering arrow. "I have seen this steed before. Iy-Joyera, the black devil. This is the king's horse. This beast has killed dozens of my best warriors and carried the murderous King of Wonderland upon his back as he burned our villages." Mundoo was now very close to Dinah, their Hornhooves dangerously close to each other as they heaved and pawed the ground, desperate to fight each other. Morte stumbled again, and Dinah lurched down toward Mundoo. The tip of his arrow brushed her throat.

"Tell me! Tell me how a dirty peasant girl has the horse of a king and the speech of a noble. Tell me now or I will spill your blood here. I will let you watch as we kill your devil, one arrow at a time." Dinah raised her chin and stared deep into the chief's eyes. She had no choice. They would no doubt kill her once they learned who she was, and it was better to die a quick death than a long one by torture. She would not go quietly, a meek, insecure princess. She would go out in a blaze of glory, a warrior who had come so far on her own, one who had made it through the Twisted Wood. She had seen death and pain, felt the blade of a sword on her neck and the thrill of the fear that preceded imminent death. She was a woman, not a girl, and she would not go without a fight.

Dinah raised her voice as she drew her sword quickly.

"My name is Dinah, and I was the future Queen of Wonderland until I escaped my father and made my way here. You will not touch my steed this day, nor spill my blood. I do not fear death from your arrows, but you should fear my sword and my rage." Morte rose up on his hind legs and she saw confusion and surprise register across Mundoo's face as she sliced her sword down toward his head. Mundoo's Hornhoov gave a skilled leap back, and Dinah swung into empty air before something hard and heavy hit the side of her head with a sickening crunch. The hazy light of the mushroom field went dim, and Dinah gave thanks that her death had been quick and painless. She closed her eyes and waited to see Charles's happy face, just on the other side of the rabbit hole.

There it was again, the swirling darkness, the inky sky, the floating clocks. Dinah twisted and turned inside it, struggling to move. Something was wrapped around her arms—a vine? No matter how much she struggled, it wrapped tighter around her, strangling her, pressing her organs uncomfortably together. She opened her mouth to scream, but the vines were in her mouth as well. Now they were the roots, the roots of the Black Towers, writhing in and out, filling her with their visions. Blood on a sword, a white ghost emerging from the darkness, its claws outstretched . . . Dinah's body jerked, and she had the sensation of falling. Then something strong and hard encircled her waist and righted her. Awareness returned and she realized that she was bobbing up and down. She shook her head once and forced her eyes to open.

Morte. She was on Morte, but what was behind her? She managed to turn her head. The Spade was sitting behind her, one arm wrapped around her waist, the other one clutching the red leather reins with desperation. She could see why. Sir Gorrann had been blindfolded. Dinah's head dropped forward, and she could see that she was bound with a heavy white rope, its texture not unlike the branches of trees. In her mouth was some sort of fabric gag, and she forced herself to breathe through her nose before she choked. The side of her head felt like a blunt object had been shoved through it, and there was dried blood crusted over her eye and nose. She tried to move her mouth and felt the Spade's hand feel its way up her face and gently remove the gag. His lips brushed against her ear, an angry rush of words pouring out.

"Do not say a word, not one godsdamn word. Yer lucky that I found a rock, otherwise you would be strewn about that field in a thousand pieces." Dinah felt the waterskin brush her lips. "Drink some water now and yeh go back to sleep. I imagine we have more than a few miles to travel before reaching Hu-Yuhar."

Dinah could barely nod her head with the thundering pain in her temple, but she managed to swallow a few gulps of water. Sir Gorrann had thrown a rock at her? Her thoughts were confused, cloudy. There were the mushrooms and the Yurkei and their arrows and then . . . she couldn't remember. Why had the Spade taken her this way in the first place?

Morte's easy lilt rocked her back to unconsciousness, and when she awoke again, the dusk was settling. She looked around. They were in a vast field of waving pale green grass, as tall as most men, interspersed with curling lavender trees that whirled and leaped from their roots. The wind rippled the grass violently from side to side, and when she tucked her head to avoid a lashing, the Yurkei didn't even seem to notice.

A line of Yurkei warriors stretched out in front of them, and Dinah noticed that she was surrounded on all sides by Yurkei guards, eyeing her and Sir Gorrann with obvious loathing. She stared back unabashedly at the warriors, so different from anything she had ever seen before. Their skin was a glowing brown, the color of wet sand. Stripes of thick white paint ran from under their eyes down their entire body, covering their arms and bare torsos. Each one had vividly blue eyes that radiated out from their dark faces. They each had white hair that came to a point in the middle of their forehead. Most had short hair, cropped to just below the neck, although Mundoo's was longer and braided down his back with stripes of blue. Each warrior wore pants (if one could call them that) made of white feathers that sat low and snug around their muscled pelvises.

They were handsome and moved with a graceful ease that eluded every human Dinah had ever known. Their horses were pale tan with white manes, smaller than the mares she had seen in the Wonderland Palace stables. Horse and rider moved as though they were of one mind. Altogether, the Yurkei created the impression of an incredible mass of terrifying skill with their quivers hanging flat across their backs, full of white arrows flecked with gray.

Mundoo rode at the front, the heavy footsteps of his Hornhoov echoing across the quiet landscape. He was taller than the rest, and Dinah could see from the rippling of muscles across his back that he was an impressive specimen. It was strange to look upon Mundoo, whose name struck fear into the heart of every Wonderland girl and boy, and see that while he was no doubt a fierce man, he was still just a man. Stories of the Yurkei ran rampant in Wonderland—stories of the horrors they inflicted upon innocent towns, of how they beat their women, of how they sacrificed their children and gnawed on human bones. It was said that they mated with cranes, and that their offspring were the terrible white bears of the Twisted Wood. Dinah had always been skeptical of the Yurkei stories—mostly because she was skeptical of everything she learned—but she could see now with her own eyes that the stories were grossly exaggerated.

These men weren't so unlike the Cards. They dressed differently and spoke in a language that sounded like the flowing of water, but they were just men, not monsters. She had learned some basic Yurkei language in her studies, but the true lesson had been unspoken: they are the enemy. *Know the language of your enemy.*

Dinah struggled against her restraints as her arms fell

asleep and her spine raged in protest from being bent forward for so many hours. "Yeh best quit moving," noted the Spade quietly. "Don't call attention to yourself."

"How are you riding Morte?" she mumbled through her gag. Even with the blindfold, she could feel Sir Gorrann's disappointment boring into her.

Finally, he gave a nod. "He let me climb up—probably because I was carrying yeh. He's heavily drugged from the mushrooms—he probably isn't even aware what's happening right now. He's just walking. Otherwise, I think he would have killed a great many today." The Spade paused. "I want to warn yeh that Morte might not live long once we get to Hu-Yuhar. Yeh must understand that he has killed many, many Yurkei."

Dinah felt her eyes blur with tears and the blood dripping from her head wound. She strained against her gag. "Whhhh . . ." Sir Gorrann pulled it out again. "Why . . . why did you lead me here?"

"Don't yeh worry about that quite yet. It will all play out." Dinah closed her eyes again, half-reassured, half-alarmed by the Spade's presence behind her. "Sleep. I'll wake yeh when we arrive. Best get yer wits about yeh. And don't try to kill the chief again, otherwise we'll both end up riddled with arrows."

I can't promise that, thought Dinah drowsily as Sir Gorrann struggled to blindly put her gag back in. *I will fight for my pathetic existence, no matter how meaningless it is at this point.* Her head throbbed, and she dropped swiftly into the soothing arms of sleep.

She awoke flat on her back, her eyes staring up at a circle of bright blue sky. She blinked a few times before her hands came up to wipe her watering eyes. Her arms were free. This was a good sign. She let her eyes play over her surroundings, hesitant to move. She was in a tent of some sort, but it wasn't triangular or square. It was perfectly round and short, shaped like the tarts she had loved back at the palace. She knew if she stood that her fingers would brush the top of the roof, and if she were just a bit taller she would be able to stick her hand through the open hole at the top. Dinah pushed herself up shakily. She was sitting on some sort of incredible mattress made of woven grass. For the first time in a long time, Dinah felt truly rested. She stretched her arms out in front of her—which led to a pulse of pain that radiated down from her head.

Tenderly, she probed the wound near her temple. Dried blood covered the area, and a lump the size of a walnut protruded from just over her ear. Her head was pounding, and the sharp pressing against her skull made her grind her teeth. She sat still for a few minutes until the sensation decreased to where she could move around. Dinah took a breath. She was fine. She was alive. It was enough. She looked longingly back at the mattress of grass and considered simply curling up and playing dead for the rest of the day, but she had a feeling that wasn't in her best interest. There were questions to be answered. Her eyes finally adjusted to the light of the tent and she saw that two Yurkei warriors stood silently near the door, their hands locked around their bows.

Dinah turned back to the mattress. A simple red tunic and a pair of white feathered pants had been laid out for her. She dressed herself quickly, vaguely aware that the warriors' bright blue eyes watched her every move, even while their faces remained unreadable. She attempted to rebraid her hair, though the thick black curtain that she once so loathed was more a rat's nest than a hairstyle these days. Her boots were gone, and she hoped that they weren't gone forever if she was going to live through all this. She had grown quite fond of wearing boots.

When she approached the door of the pod-shaped room, the two guards parted. "Mundoo wish to see you," said one of them in heavily accented Wonderlander. Dinah nodded, hoping they couldn't sense her growing fear. *They haven't killed me yet*, she told herself. *That's something.* The seething hatred in one guard's blue eyes was intense, while the other looked simply intrigued by her presence. Taking a breath, she pulled back the tent flap. White sunlight assaulted her eyes as Dinah struggled to comprehend what she was seeing. After a few moments, she let herself exhale, stunned into a respectful silence. She was in Hu-Yuhar, the legendary city of the Yurkei. She stood in a very narrow valley surrounded by rocky gray cliff faces on both sides that veered up and away. Past these towering walls of stone, the gorgeous Yurkei Mountains rose up around them, their tops always concealed behind a foggy mist that rolled and leaped like a child at play. The mountains were said to be endless, and the closer Dinah got to them the more she believed it.

The entire valley couldn't have been more than half a mile wide. The ground was covered by a lush, bluish-green grass. Horses were everywhere, roaming free—eating, running, sleeping. The valley floor seemed to belong to them, although she watched hundreds of Yurkei going about their daily business on two narrow dirt pathways flanking the rock walls. Dinah looked up, shielding her eyes from the light that draped the whole valley in dewy sunshine. Tents—shaped just like the one she had awakened in—protruded from the mountainside, hovering above the ground like little clouds. Round and flat, they jutted out from holes in the rock or the edges of cliffs or, sometimes, just the vertical, flat rock face. Long wooden beams that twisted and wrapped under the pods secured each tent to the side of the mountain, supporting them from below. *Biscuits*, thought Dinah, that's what the shape reminded her of. Round, flat biscuits.

Soaring through the space between the two mountain faces was a system of lofty bridges, made of the same wooden material that secured the tents to the cliff sides. Yurkei moved across the bridges with alarming speed: children chasing each other, women walking swiftly with baskets full of food, men dashing around carrying handfuls of arrows. The valley bustled with life, although most of it was taking place above Dinah's head. Something hit her shoulder, something blunt and hard. She winced and turned around. The Yurkei warrior who had looked at her with such loathing stood behind her, brandishing the butt of a long, curved spear. "You. Move. To chief."

Dinah began walking forward, not sure of where she was going until several Yurkei children ran in front of her and proceeded to lead the way. Their long white hair flowed freely over their shoulders, clean of the white stripes that marked the men. Boy or girl, Dinah found it hard to tell. Altogether they were lovely, until one of them turned and spat in her face.

"C'hallgu quon!" Then several others turned and followed suit. "C'hallgu quon! C'hallgu quon!" they chanted. *Bad queen?* Dinah tried to translate in her mind as she wiped the spit off her lip. Small rocks appeared out of nowhere and suddenly Dinah was being pelted with all kinds of things: grass, rocks, spit, and dirt. She raised her hands to protect herself and the two Yurkei guards closed in on her, each taking one arm and barking orders at the children. Fervently, she looked around for Sir Gorrann, but his grizzled face was nowhere to be seen. She was alone.

On the sides of the valley, Yurkei women had lined up to watch her, this dirty and humiliated princess. She tripped over her feet as they stared, and she felt even more humbled by their wild beauty and piercing stares. The women wore only white feathered skirts that draped loosely around their legs and a white feathered band that covered their breasts. Each woman was muscled and lean, with smooth dark skin and shining blue eyes. Their hair was long and twisted back into several elaborate buns accented by sparse blue beads that winked in the sunlight. Dinah felt so out of place, a hideous monster with her pale white skin, black hair, and black eyes. Their eyes narrowed as she passed. The tunic was given to her with a purpose, she realized. She was wearing red, the color of Wonderland Palace, a color to remind those around her exactly who she was. Red, the color of blood, the color of the oppressor. *I should have gone naked*, she thought, stumbling again. *I might have attracted less notice.*

The crowds parted in front of her as she approached a massive white rope ladder that seemed to hang in midair. Dinah glanced up, her neck straining to take in its height. Far above, carved out of the two mighty rock walls that lined the valley, two cranes faced each other—their wings outstretched, their chests puffed out. Two long necks elongated into huge heads with terrible, open beaks. The carvings were so large that the beaks were almost touching, though they began on opposite sides of the valley.

"Meir hu-gofrey," murmured the Yurkei warrior who had looked at her with such curiosity. "Our protectors and gods." Dinah nodded. She knew that the Yurkei worshipped the birds, and that Wonderland's fascination with birds had grown out of their early meetings with the Yurkei. A single large pod was suspended between the birds, harnessed by the same wooden supports she had seen in the valley. The chief lived there, she guessed, ruling his people from between two warring birds, each the size of a foothill.

Dinah stopped and stared at the ladder. It blew about in the wind, looking weak and worn. "I can't."

The angry Yurkei warrior pushed Dinah up to the

ladder and placed her hand on the bottom rung.

"Climb," he demanded.

Dinah looked up. The pod was suspended hundreds of feet above the earth. A fall from even the middle would surely either kill her or break every bone in her body. She took a deep breath and began making her way up the rope ladder that somehow blew in the breeze but still managed to be strong and unbendable beneath her white-knuckled grip. Hand over hand, she made her way up with the two Yurkei warriors lingering behind her, obviously annoyed by how slowly she was climbing. A strong gust of wind rocked the ladder, and Dinah pressed herself against it, wrapping her arms and legs around the rungs. She heard the roaring laughter of Yurkei children from below who watched her desperately cling to the ladder for dear life as it lifted off the ground and blew out behind the warriors, lashing like an angry tail.

"Up, up!" shouted the guard behind her. Dinah clutched the ladder, afraid to move. The ladder twisted and swayed, and Dinah let out a cry before murmuring nearly forgotten prayers from childhood as she clutched the rung before her. The ladder began to twirl in the wind, which cracked and whistled the faster it blew. The rung underneath her hand was growing slippery with sweat, and Dinah's foot was tangled between two other rungs. *I can't*, she thought.

Before she could finish her thought, the kinder of the two guards began rapidly climbing up the ladder after her. He reached her in seconds. Once there, he moved slowly, circling around the ladder until he was on the opposite side, his face inches from Dinah's. He dangled from the rope with one hand as he untangled Dinah's footing with the other. He switched hands then and wrapped one palm around the wooden rope and the other tightly around her waist. "I will help," he murmured. "Step."

Dinah closed her eyes and reached for the next rung, secured by his hand supporting her waist. Her foot found the rung. She opened her eyes. Without thinking, she grabbed the next rung and the one after that, even when the wind wrenched the ladder sideways so roughly that Dinah almost lost her grip. The Yurkei warrior held on to her as she slipped and strained her way up. At times it seemed hopeless, but still she climbed. She climbed up past the breasts of the enormous cranes, past the crests of their giant necks, and finally, straight up into the vast white pod strung between the two birds, like some saucer that the fowl had dropped from their mouths.

The Yurkei warrior was the first one through the pod, and he rapped his hand twice against a wooden bracket on the outside. A square of fabric was pulled from the bottom, and with a leap, he disappeared up into the hole, reaching back to help Dinah. Her feet dangled in the air as he held her arms, and she looked up with fear into his glowing blue eyes, her life completely in his hands. He gave her a shy smile and yanked her up through the opening, setting her down roughly inside the tent. Dinah's legs and arms were shaking so terribly that she simply rolled over onto her back, her lungs heaving and contracting with each long breath. Her hands wouldn't stop trembling, a cold sweat pouring from her skin. It felt good to be on a hard surface, but she couldn't forget that this fabric tent was suspended hundreds of feet in the air. It was unnatural to be this high, and she longed to feel dirt underneath her fingernails. She was a child of the earth, not the sky. Her heart gave a terrified thud when she realized that she would also have to climb back down the ladder, which would be less physically exhausting but infinitely more dangerous. She closed her eyes and focused on breathing. After a few minutes, a man's voice broke the silence.

"Did you enjoy your climb, Princess?" Warily, Dinah opened her eyes and pushed herself into a sitting position. She tried to force her heaving breaths down into her ribs, to appear more in control. Mundoo stood before her, looking resplendent in a full headdress made of blue feathers, wearing nothing more than a feathered loincloth and some sort of wooden sandal that laced up the ankle and calf. The white painted stripes she had seen on him before were gone, now replaced with elaborately illustrated white drawings and symbols that coated his skin. He sat calmly on a huge throne of carved golden birds that, much to her surprise, was not unlike the Heart thrones in the Great Hall. In fact, the more she looked at it, the more she realized it was the twin of the thrones in Wonderland Palace. Carved by the same maker at the same time, no doubt.

Stand up, Dinah told herself. *You look weak*. She forced

herself shakily to her feet and raised her head. Mundoo stood and motioned to his guards. "Lu-feryir." The guards turned and walked toward several open flaps around the bean-shaped tent and out into the open air. Dinah gasped before realizing her foolishness when she saw that the ropes suspending the pod high above the earth were also slim walkways leading into tunnels, carved out from the breasts of the stone birds.

"Would you like some water? The ladder climb can be . . . strenuous for those who aren't used to it." Dinah waved his water away. She didn't want anything from him except for mercy, though her throat longed for liquid.

"The ladder climb was to make me look weak." She raised her chin. "Your Majesty."

Mundoo gave a small laugh. "You know, you don't remind me of your father, not much. Your pride and your blatant lack of self-control, perhaps. But otherwise . . ." He peered into her dark eyes. "I do not see the man in you who has killed so many of my own."

Dinah lowered her eyes. "My father, the king, murdered my brother in cold blood so that he would not have to share the crown. I have no love for my father and the fact that you see none of him in me is the greatest compliment I've ever been paid."

Mundoo smiled and lifted his hand to Dinah's cheek. She forced herself to stay steady as his tan, weathered hand caressed her jawline. "And what of Wonderland Palace? Do you have loyalty to them? To the Cards?"

Dinah considered her answer carefully. *I am a mouse in an eagle's nest*, she thought, *and one wrong move will deliver me straight into his mouth.* "I have no loyalty to Wonderland while it remains under the rule of the man who murdered my brother."

Mundoo's bright blue eyes sparkled. "Well answered. I see you are adept at the language of ruling and politics. I should not be surprised." Mundoo stepped back from her and began pacing around his throne. "You must know the history of my people and Wonderland. Our legends say that the Yurkei arrived here hundreds of years ago, flown here on the backs of great birds. We lived in peace with the land, and made this place—Hu-Yuhar, the hidden city—our home. We had no need for war, for weapons, other than to hunt. And then one day, strangers came, borne by a boat from a distant land, from the 'Other Worlds' as you call them. These men established Wonderland Palace and proceeded to push us back into the mountains. Your ancestors declared war on us, and we have been battling the line of Hearts ever since.

"And for what? We long for nothing more than to live on our lands and have peace. It's true—when a Wonderland village comes too close to our lands, we will burn it to the ground, because we must fight for each inch of grass. This is a vast country, and yet the palace feels it must own every inch of it, from the Western Sea to the edge of the Yurkei Mountains. As you are probably well aware, I have spies in Wonderland Palace, and I hear whispers that your father is laying the groundwork to start his great war. He longs to push us into the sea, the place from where his ancestors came. He seeks to find and destroy Hu-Yuhar."

Mundoo gave a sigh and rested his hand upon the throne as he gazed at her. Dinah could see lines of worry etched across his strong face. "And so we come to you, you who rode so boldly into my territory astride the black devil. What do I do with an exiled princess? Most of the people down there would have you publicly executed." Dinah stood still as Mundoo raised a few flaps on the side of the tent. Then he wrapped his hand around her neck and pushed her face toward the light. "Look down, Dinah. You may have been exiled from Wonderland and the king himself may wish you dead, but that matters little to a fatherless child or a woman whose bed will never be warm again."

Dinah kept quiet as she looked down at the throngs of people below, Mundoo's hand against the back of her head. Nothing he said was untrue.

"Executing you, your Spade, and your steed would be the easiest course of action. But I think that we can find a better use for you. How much do you know of your kingdom as it currently stands?"

"I know that the city is restless because of raised taxes. I know that my father is growing ever more paranoid and that he is amassing the Cards in great numbers; for what purpose, I am unsure. I know that he has placed Vittiore, his puppet, on the throne next to him, and that he rules with an ever harder iron fist. He is preparing for something, but it is of little concern to me. I am no longer a member of the royal family. I am now simply a girl who has no home."

Mundoo smiled. "If only I could believe that. I hear your sister is very beautiful, with hair like the sun."

"And a mind like mud," replied Dinah, sharper than she intended. "She does nothing that my father does not tell her to do. Vittiore could not rule over an anthill."

"Interesting. But your father, he is a clever man, no?"

Dinah thought of how her father had beheaded Faina Baker right in front of her just to teach her to not put her nose where it didn't belong. "He is intelligent, yes. He is a skilled fighter, but he is also brutal and unforgiving and a drunk. It has made him slow in recent years. He is full of hatred, for reasons I do not understand. The cleverest man in the palace is Cheshire. Most of the decisions my father makes come from him." In her mind's eye, Dinah saw Charles's tiny body crumpled under a starry sky. Her voice rose. "I have nothing but hatred for the king. I would gladly take his life. I attempted to in the Twisted Wood until the Spade intervened."

"So I have heard." Mundoo stared at her, his unflinching blue eyes piercing her tingling bones. "I find you very interesting, Dinah, exiled Princess of Wonderland. Stories of your escape from the palace have echoed through this land, even here in Hu-Yuhar, our home. You are called many things: the Queen of Death, the Red Queen, the Rebel Queen, Rider of the Black Devil. Some even say you are a ghost or an omen of the future. . . ."

"I am no one," replied Dinah. "I am simply Dinah, an exile who stumbled into your mushroom fields by accident."

Mundoo raised his eyebrow. "By accident? Yes, that *is* interesting. No one stumbles into our sacred burial ground by accident. No. Your Spade led you there, though his reasons are not yet clear."

"No, we were . . . " Dinah found the words dying on her tongue, and the twinge in her heart told her that Mundoo was right. The Spade had led her there. *Had she known it the whole time, exchanging her own security for the comfort of a friend?* She had thought they were simply fleeing the king, perhaps heading over the Yurkei Mountains to the Other Worlds. "I trusted him," she gasped, her throat dry and raspy.

Mundoo stood and handed her a small wooden bowl

filled with water. "Drink. I insist. It pains me to hear your voice."

Dinah, feeling humbled, gulped the water noisily.

"You should know not to trust anyone when you possess so much power."

"I do not possess power," she answered, wiping her mouth. "I possess a sword, a bag full of filthy clothing, the pelt of a white bear, and a horse."

"Ah, your horse." Mundoo untied a piece of fabric that was lashed to his glorious throne and the roof of the tent pulled back, like an egg with its shell removed. The sky opened up above them, and the space was filled with the whirling cold wind that had so easily tossed the ladder. Dinah barely had time to duck before a giant white crane flapped into the tent, its huge wings sending bursts of air across her face. The crane landed on the throne and gave a loud squawk at Dinah. Mundoo continued, seemingly oblivious to the dangerous-looking bird. "Morte will be put to death soon enough. A price must be paid for all the blood he has taken from this tribe. Believe that I will find no joy in killing a Hornhoov. They are rare and exquisite creatures, and I have never seen one as large as him. We will study him first."

"He hasn't done anything." Dinah knew it was untrue as soon as the words passed over her tongue.

"No? With my own eyes, I saw him crush three of my best warriors without even a backward glance—at least, not until he came back to taste their flesh." Dinah remembered the bear, Morte's muzzle covered with the smear of blood, and the way her stomach had turned. "The beast *will* die. And then we shall decide what to do with his rider. I have much to think about. My spies have given me reason to believe that your father is preparing to launch a large assault on my tribe, perhaps bringing the fight here, to Hu-Yuhar, within a few months' time."

"But your city seems impregnable. It is surrounded by mountains on every side."

Mundoo smiled as the crane rested its head on his knee. "So one would think, but I do not underestimate your father. We have our weaknesses, just like any city. But that is for me to consider. For now, you will stay here as our guest. You will attend our feasts and ceremonies, and I would encourage you to talk with our tribe, to learn. You may not leave the valley, and you may not enter any homes. You are to keep up your training with the Spade, and I will command my strongest warrior to help give you instruction and build your skills. You are not to go near Morte. And if he suddenly disappears or is set free, you die, along with the Spade. I will make you watch as we take him piece by piece."

"Where is Sir Gorrann?"

"He will be waiting for you back at your tent. We spoke earlier this morning, and he handled the climb even worse than you did." Dinah's mouth curved into the smallest of smiles as Mundoo strolled up behind her. At least Sir Gorrann was alive. "We will speak again, Princess, but for now you must go. You have met your guards, Ki-ershan and Yur-Jee. They will follow you wherever you go. Yur-Jee lost his eldest son to your father's Heartsword, so I would be careful not to anger him. Passion can lead a man to violent ways."

Dinah nodded and turned to go. The sunlight winked in front of her face, just for a second, and then there was an arm around her neck, a body pressed against her back. Mundoo had moved so fast. Dinah didn't understand what was happening. The pain came swiftly as something sharp and hard was shoved into her, through her. Her shoulder exploded, and everything went white. She grasped his outstretched hand, where she saw a thin wooden knife made of the same white wood that held the tent aloft. It was as slender as a knitting needle, and now covered with red. Mundoo took a breath and shoved it into her back again, just over her shoulder blade. *He was killing her.* She didn't feel it going in, but the pain when it was pulled out was worse than anything she had ever felt. Dinah let out a muffled scream as the blood rushed forth over her shoulder. The pain was deep, like a thousand scalding irons were being pushed inside her. She stumbled backward before falling to her knees with a choking gasp. Mundoo knelt behind her and wrapped his thick arm around her neck again, his lips brushing her ear as he pulled her close. Dinah gurgled and choked. His hand was covered in blood.

"Don't be afraid, Princess. It's not a fatal wound I've given you, and it will heal quickly. That was for swinging your sword at my head. I am the noble chief of the Yurkei and a man of honor, and I wouldn't want you to think that we were friends." His hot breath lingered over her face, and she felt herself spiraling into his glowing blue eyes, losing consciousness. "You and I, we are both the blood of Wonderland. It flows from my people and through your veins. I can't let you forget it."

He released her violently, and she fell face forward onto the wooden floor of the tent, writhing in pain. The chief called for Ki-ershan and Yur-Jee, and they appeared through one of the open flaps of the tent door.

"Take her through the mountain," Mundoo instructed with a wave of his hand. "Make sure no one hurts her or the Spade until I have made a decision regarding their fates. Feed, clean, and clothe them. See that they are well cared for but closely watched. Call for Ge-Jursi to use Iu-Hora's potions to heal her." Dinah's whole body curled up in blinding pain as she cried out. Yur-Jee raised his voice to argue with the chief, but Mundoo silenced him. "Do as I command. Ach-julik."

Yur-Jee bowed with his hands spread out before him into the symbol of the crane. Dinah's guards pulled her out through one of the tent's open doors. She gasped for air, unable to breathe through the pain. They pushed her out onto the rope walkway that led into the breast of the crane. Dinah stumbled repeatedly, which made treading on the thin, knotted-rope walkway even more terrifying. Blood dripped down from her shoulder until it coated her bare feet, and she struggled to stay conscious. She slipped. Ki-ershan pressed his palm over the wound to stop the bleeding. Dinah could see the ground hundreds of feet below her as they struggled to stay on the thin rope bridge. The crowd watched her in silence as drops of blood fell from her body. They seemed satisfied.

"Walk," grunted Yur-Jee, roughly pushing her forward, so hard that Dinah would have gone flying off the edge if Ki-ershan hadn't yanked her back. "Ja-hohy!" he snapped at Yur-Jee. *Stop*, thought Dinah, half-delusional. *Yes, ja-hohy means* stop. *Thank you, Harris*, she thought madly.

Something twitched in her shoulder and suddenly it felt as if the bone was separating from her muscle, somewhere deep inside the cut. She gave a scream and stumbled forward, her knees hitting the rock outcropping that led into the mountain. Overjoyed at the cool feel of the stone, she laughed hysterically. The urge to brush her lips on the mountain was overtaken by a throbbing, angry pain. She heard raised voices and shouting. Sir Gorrann's face appeared in a hazy blue sky over her, the thin lines of his face creased in worry.

"Yer Highness, let me see." His hands cradled her face, her shoulder. The Spade turned her over gently, peeling Kiershan's hand back from the wound, and she heard a sharp intake of breath. "Yur-Jee, please get me some bandages and a healer. *Now!*"

Dinah closed her eyes. When she opened them again, there was a beautiful Yurkei woman leaning over her, her glowing blue eyes trained on Dinah's wound, her flowing white hair soaked red at the tips where it had brushed in her blood. She listened silently as the woman sang a wailing song over her, rocked back and forth, and applied some sort of gray paste to Dinah's wound. The paste smelled like the mushroom fields—warm and potent, a decadent perfume. The pain suddenly receded into a dull, stabbing sensation, and Dinah breathed a sigh of relief, her hand reaching up to clutch the woman's shoulder. "Thank you, thank you, thank you." She repeated it over and over, her tongue becoming numb.

The woman smiled, showing her small pearly teeth. "How do you say . . . in Wonderlander? Su-heyg . . . hu-sang . . ." The woman clapped her hands. "Oh yes, hu-satey." Her blue eyes stared unflinchingly into Dinah's. "Welcome to Hu-Yuhar."

Eight

Dinah slept for two glorious days on the bed of woven grass. Occasionally, she would be awoken by the pain. She'd eat and relieve herself before surrendering to sleep. Sir Gorrann sat quietly beside her bed, always watchful. He must have slept, but Dinah didn't know when he did, and she didn't really care. The healing paste made her dreams vivid and joyful. Charles, weaving feathers into a hat. Harris, adjusting his spectacles while they feasted on wine and grapes. Wardley, astride Corning, his brown hair glowing like warm choco-late in the sun, his arms reaching for her. Wardley . . . she thought of him often in the few minutes between waking and falling back asleep. Wardley, her love, whom she probably would never see again. Wardley the Weak, as he was called now. The shame she felt at tarnishing his name was at times unbearable, so it was easier just to sleep.

When two days had finally passed, Dinah begrudgingly decided that it was time to leave the confines of her warm, cozy tent. Sir Gorrann roused her early and made sure that she ate a plate of eggs and strange amber fruit. As Dinah bit into the egg, a rush of yellow yolk ran down her chin. She stared at Sir Gorrann, who was devouring his eggs.

"Did you lead me here?" she asked. The Spade wiped his face with a feathered napkin.

"Perhaps. Perhaps it is not yet time to ask."

Dinah flung her plate across the room with a fury that surprised even herself. Her wound screamed in protest and she let out a tiny whimper. "Why? Why would you take us here?"

The Spade stood and brushed off his lap. "I'll not answer that question now, not while yeh are acting like a child. But I would say, ask yerself if yeh trust me. You'll find the answer is yes, I think. That's really for you to decide. But for right now, I think we should take yeh down to the river to bathe because I have never seen anyone look so disgusting, and your wound will need washing and re-dressing."

He left the tent without another word. Dinah stewed for a few minutes in the bright white light of the tent. He had led her here. But why? To provide the Yurkei with the revenge they so desired? To ransom her off to the king, who would then kill her? No matter how many situations she came up with, not a single one of them made any sense. The Spade had saved her, protected her, taught her to fight. One did not give one's enemy a sword and instruct the arm to wield it.

Finally, with a cry of pain and a stream of curses that would make the Spade proud, Dinah sat up and pulled a tunic over her head. She ducked out of the tent to find Ki-ershan waiting for her. He nodded his head toward a dirt path that ran behind her tent. "Thank you," she whispered. He smiled back at her. Ki-ershan was definitely her favorite of the two guards. He followed behind as Dinah proceeded to walk slowly down the path until she arrived at a tiny freshwater stream that ran the length of the valley. Her wound still pulsed with pain, but it was nothing compared to the pain she remembered from the wooden knife. Sir Gorrann waited for her at a bend in the trail, and they walked together in silence toward the bank.

She stopped at the stream and stared into the water. It was small, barely ten feet across, but it gurgled and danced in the morning sun, its water so clear that it was almost like looking in a mirror. Dinah had thought she had no embarrassment left after being paraded through the valley in her bright red tunic and then forced to climb the ladder into the sky, but she had been wrong. In the shiny blue stream, there were hundreds of Yurkei bathing, playing, and washing clothing. The women all bathed naked, their perfect lean bodies glistening in the sun. Dinah saw Sir Gorrann glance away, a red flush rising in his cheeks. Dinah slowly undressed herself, trying to cover all that she could with her tunic before lowering herself quickly into the icy water with a wince as it converged on her wound. All eyes watched her as she came up, no doubt disgusted at this pale, bruised creature with black hair and the darkest eyes they had ever seen.

The intense cold took her breath away and she immediately started shivering. Sir Gorrann climbed in after her, struggling to cover himself as well, giving his own gasp at the cold water. He dunked his head and then emerged, shaking the water out of his gray hair. He then began to scrub her wound with fervor. The moment was anything but intimate, as they were both freezing and working as quickly as possible.

Sir Gorrann raised his voice. "Yer wound . . . it's almost healed. I've never seen anything like it." Indeed, her wound was closing nicely after two days of rest, and whatever healing paste had been put on it had sealed it shut. Her shoulder had a constant ache, and when she raised her arms there was a thin slice of pain. Mundoo had left her a scar, a remembrance of him. Dinah watched as the clean water around her became cloudy with the dirt and muck scrubbed from her skin. There was something in the gentle way the Spade touched her shoulder, something that made Dinah realize that even though he had led them into the mouth of the Yurkei, she deeply trusted him. He would never hurt her. She knew it instinctively, the same way she knew the stars would change each night. Sir Gorrann cursed the chief as he scrubbed at the scabbed wound.

"He believed yeh deserved this, no doubt, but it didn't have to be so deep. What with the coming battles . . . ?"

"Why should it matter?" replied Dinah. "There are plenty of people here who would like to see my head on a stake, sooner rather than later."

"The Yurkei don't behead," said Sir Gorrann calmly as he dunked his head again under the stream. "They drop their prisoners from the wings of the cranes onto the stones below." He stopped, suddenly aware of what that image would do to Dinah. "I'm sorry, Yer Highness. I forgot."

She spread her fingers in the water, seeing Charles on the stone slab. "Don't be sorry. It would be fitting to die like my brother." Dinah was suddenly aware that the noisy stream had grown very silent. The Yurkei women were climbing naked out of the water and gathering up their children with whispered words of compliance. The children struggled, unhappy to have their playtime cut short, but the women carried them away. Noting the sudden exodus of bathers, Dinah felt compelled to grab for her red tunic, pulling it into the water and wriggling into it like a fish. Within seconds, Dinah and Sir Gorrann were the only ones left in the stream. Dinah heard the crunch of branches behind her and turned, her arms wrapped tightly across her chest, her heart thudding beneath them.

Two huge feet stood before her on the bank—gnarled, gross feet—slabs of meat marked with calluses and scars. They led up to the tallest man Dinah had ever seen. It was strange seeing someone with a similar skin tone to hers here, in the depths of Yurkei country. His hair was a honeyed brown rather than white, though it was long and cut in the Yurkei manner. It came to a downward point on his forehead, his eyes a dull green. A jagged scar ran from his chin up past his cheek, mingling with the white stripes of paint that trailed from just under his eye to his shins. He wore only a feather loincloth. Thighs and arms like tree trunks stretched out from his rigid torso. He would dwarf even her father. In one hand he clutched an elaborately curved bow and arrow. In the other was a Heartsword.

Dinah's stomach gave a lurch when she saw the sunlight flicker off the double-sided blade. Only her father and the highest-ranking Cards carried Heartswords. She stared in wonder, her arms pressed tightly over her chest. The man glowered at them before throwing his weapons on the bank. Without warning, he reached down and plucked Dinah straight out of the water by clasping both of her arms at her side and lifting, as easily as if he had picked up a rag doll. Something felt as if it was ripping inside her shoulder. She struggled, but it was no use. His grip was as strong as iron. Her feet dangled above the ground. Sir Gorrann rushed to climb out of the stream, his eyes on the man.

The man sneered as he looked into Dinah's surprised face. "This skinny dark-eyed girl is the great Princess of Wonderland? The one who bested her father, stole his horse, and left a bloody trail behind her? It can't be. You are barely the size of my thigh and weak as a newly hatched worm. Are you this legendary warrior, the Rebel Queen?"

Dinah strained her neck to look up at him, water streaming into her eyes. Her mouth seemed unable to form words.

"Speak up!" he bellowed, his breath blowing her hair back. Dinah bit her lip, the fury inside her poking its head out of slumber. She twisted to free herself, but it was of no use. Instead she fixed her black eyes on his.

"I am Dinah, the former Princess of Wonderland. This is my guard, Sir Gorrann, a Spade, and one of the most feared trackers in the Cards."

"So I have heard," he said. "A wet mouse and her old man guardian; this is who I am to train?" With a laugh, he set her down on the ground.

Dinah raised her chin. "And your name?"

"You can call me Bah-kan. As you may have noticed, I do not look like most of my brothers here in Hu-Yuhar." He grinned. "My given name is Stern Ravier and I was once the highest-ranking Club Card in the king's army."

Dinah let out a gasp. There were poems and stories about the bravest Club that had ever lived—in fact, his giant statue had lorded over Charles's room.

"You're famous," she stuttered, her lips blue with cold. "And dead!"

The huge man let out a bellow that seemed to rustle the trees around them. "So Wonderland Palace would have you believe. My Yurkei name, the true name you will call me, is

Bah-kan, which means the Tall Warrior. I am here to train you." His eyes traveled over Dinah's form. "You have my permission to dry yourself."

Dinah staggered over to her white feathered pants, as light as a whisper when she pulled them over her stinging wet skin and soaked tunic. Sir Gorrann stood nearby, his hands covering his groin as he eyed Bah-kan.

"Stories of your mighty death resound in the halls of the Cards," he said forcefully. "How is it that you are now a Yurkei warrior, though you bear the highest honors of Wonderland Palace?" His tone was accusing. *Traitor.*

"Ah, that's a story for another time. For now, we must go. Mundoo insists that training begin today, for both of you." He gave Sir Gorrann a hard slap on the shoulder. "It's good to see another Card, even if it must be a Spade. It's a wonder you kept her alive. Spades aren't exactly known for their abilities."

Sir Gorrann lunged toward Bah-kan, who brought down his palm straight against the Spade's chest without flinching. Sir Gorrann flew back into the stream as if he was thrown there by the gods. He surfaced with a furious look on his face, water streaming from his gray hair. Dinah tried to control it, but laughter was churning its way up her throat and before long she was laughing so hysterically that she was doubled over. Tears reddened her eyes. The whole situation, everything, was so terrible, so strange and confusing. And yet she could only laugh at Sir Gorrann simmering in the water, looking like a drowned cat. The giant Yurkei warrior standing guard laughed quietly to himself as she quickly pulled her hair into a low bun.

Bah-kan cleared his throat. "I'm glad to give you a laugh, Princess. Your training will commence in a few minutes. Follow this path by the river, turn right at the waterfall, and then come to a rest in front of the livestock pen, just below the knee of the crane." He wiggled his eyebrows. "I heard from Mundoo that you have the fiery blood of your father. Personally, I can't wait to find out." Bah-kan gathered up his weapons and stomped off. Normally this sort of insult would have sent Dinah into a rage, but instead it made her laugh harder. Eventually, the Spade relaxed as well, chuckling while he floated on his back in the stream, spitting water into the air. It was a good while before they trekked their way back to the valley floor, when Dinah raised her voice. "Why are they training me to fight? What good could that possibly do?"

The Spade was silent for a moment. "Well, at least they aren't killing yeh."

Dinah began laughing again. It was all so . . . *strange*.

Unfortunately, the laughter didn't last. Bah-kan was a brutal fighter and a merciless trainer. He had no stomach for weakness and made a game out of fighting them with one hand—and sometimes with no hands.

Crowds of Yurkei gathered around them each morning to watch Bah-kan humiliate and exploit their weaknesses. The focus was on Dinah, but he also sparred with Sir Gorrann several times a day. Those fights were incredible to watch, and Dinah felt that she learned more from watching those than when she herself was training. Even Mundoo, who took mysterious journeys into the mountain tunnels during the day, made rare appearances to watch the fights.

Swords flew and clanged through the valley, the swift dance of warriors, one that attracted even the best Yurkei warriors to watch and dissect. Bah-kan would preempt the

Spade's strokes and parry with his own, the Heartsword close to his breast to act as both shield and weapon. Sir Gorrann was the more cautious of the two, the more calculating. He saved his advances for those times when he had the best opportunities. Bah-kan had the advantage of strength, but he also was an intelligent fighter, one who weighed challenging maneuvers before charging in with fearless abandon. They were well matched. There were several times when Dinah feared Sir Gorrann would lose his life, when Bah-kan's blade came a little too close, but he always leaped out of the way at the ideal moment, or cried to yield.

Bah-kan was unstoppable, she realized, perhaps the best warrior she had ever seen in her life. He was the lethal combination of a highly disciplined Card mixed with the best traits of a Yurkei warrior—equal parts brutal and graceful, moving as if he was dancing on air. Dinah realized quickly that there were none in Wonderland or Yurkei country that could best him, aside from perhaps Xavier Juflee, the Knave of Hearts. But she wasn't sure that even he could beat Bah-kan.

Dinah and Bah-kan sparring was much less exciting,

since it took only a few minutes before Dinah was facedown on the ground, beaten and exhausted in every possible way. Still, she was proud that she could meet most of his blows with a somewhat broad counterstrike of her own. She was no longer swinging into the air with large, heavy-handed strokes but rather with quick strikes of her blade combined with rapid foot movement. She danced around Bah-kan, and once managed to land a hard blow just above his ribs that left him gasping. The Yurkei surrounding them had whooped and stomped their feet.

Bah-kan gave a tiny laugh and then plunged forward, rage playing across his white-striped face. Dinah jumped high to avoid a low stroke and brought the butt of her blade down hard on his knee. It was like striking a rock, and the vibrations that shot through her once-broken fingers made her wince in pain. Bah-kan was upon her then. He swung the Heartsword across her chest but stopped mid-swing, twisted around, and punched her in the back of the shoulder—right in the spot where Mundoo had sunk his thin blade. She screamed.

"Bah-kan!" shouted Sir Gorrann, angry.

Bah-kan shrugged. "An enemy will look for her obvious weakness. Why shouldn't I?"

Surprised by the white-hot pain blowing through her shoulder and distracted by rage, Dinah swung her sword at his arm. It was a mistake. He caught the blade with the end of his Heartsword and wrenched backward. Dinah's sword went sailing into the crowd and she was left empty-handed.

"Your Highness!" Dinah looked up just in time to see Sir Gorrann toss his knife in her direction. She caught it and turned to meet Bah-kan again. The crowd was silent as Bah-kan shifted his weight from foot to foot, as if thinking of a million ways to kill her. Bah-kan spoke.

"Your father, the King of Wonderland, is a whoremonger and a cheat." The Yurkei cheered at his words.

Dinah clasped her hand around the dagger. "I agree!" she yelled back.

The crowd laughed, and Bah-kan let a smile draw across his face. "Your half sister is a dozen times more beautiful than you. I hear she is a good queen."

Dinah felt the fury rising up inside of her, the clawing black heat that she so often pushed back down. Still, she remained calm. "You are surely right. She is lovely, even though she is a false queen."

Bah-kan sidestepped and then charged, his Heartsword raised as if to carve her in half. Dinah rolled in front of him, clipping him at the shins and making him tumble. As she passed, she nicked the back of his calf with her dagger. Bah-kan roared as he landed, and Dinah scurried to her feet, the dagger poised to throw. For a second, she had the advantage. Bah-kan was distracted by his bleeding leg, and the Heartsword was down. The voice barreling down insults continued.

"Your mother was just as well-known for her whoring as she was for her mad son."

Dinah screamed with rage as the fury overtook her and she flung the knife at Bah-kan. The blade was thrown so sloppily that it bounced off the edge of his Heartsword even though he never moved it. With inhuman speed, he reached out, caught it in his hands, and flung it back at Dinah. She watched as it buried itself deep in her chest armor. Without the armor that Mundoo insisted upon, she would have been dead, but that was the least of her cares. Seeing nothing but her all-encompassing black rage, she launched herself upon Bah-kan and ripped at his ear with her teeth.

"Your Highness! Dinah! Stop!" She felt Sir Gorrann grab her waist and tug her back.

Bah-kan shoved her off with one hand. "Control her! Gods, there's a fire in this one!" The crowd stared as Sir Gorrann carried her, squirming and screaming, back to her tent.

That had been a dark day, but the training continued. Each and every morning her lesson was learned: when she let her fury get the best of her, she lost control of herself, her fight, and her focus. She learned to remain calm and in control and told herself that revenge was best taken with a blade—not a violent tantrum. Bah-kan's strength and skill always bested her in the end, and would forever, but Dinah grew exponentially as a fighter each time his Heartsword met her blade. Between the training that Wardley had given her growing up, the time she had spent learning from Sir Gorrann in the woods, and the brutal, one-on-one fighting with Bah-kan, Dinah felt increasingly more comfortable with the blade in her hand. The next day, she faced off sword to sword with a dozen different Yurkei warriors, and more often than not, they fought as equals.

After their seventh day of training, Bah-kan released Dinah early, saying that he had to visit his wife and brood of children, who lived at the other end of the valley. Dinah smiled at the thought—Bah-kan and his Yurkei wife, and their tent full of monstrous children, all taller than the rest of the Yurkei children, with white hair and shining blue eyes.

Dinah yawned as she rested her sword up against a wooden paddock, noting that even the fence posts had been carved with tiny winged birds. Her muscles quivered with exhaustion as she made her way toward her tent, fancying the bed that waited for her. As she pushed back the tent flap, she bumped hard into Sir Gorran's chest. "You can't come here now, girl." She stepped back, annoyance playing across her face.

"I'm exhausted. Get out of my way." She tried to push past him and ended up being flung backward.

He tipped an invisible hat at her. "Doesn't matter where you go, but you can't come in here. Perhaps wander the valley, or find a ripe dinner in the orchard."

Dinah sighed, too tired to argue with him. "Fine. Enjoy your company."

Sir Gorrann clicked his tongue and winked. Dinah rolled her eyes, but sadly walked away from the tent, rubbing her aching neck and dreaming of a pillow. She suspected his pressing appointment was with one of the Yurkei women who was fond of watching him bathe every day, but it wasn't worth mentioning. After the life he had endured, perhaps Sir Gorrann deserved some momentary happiness. Dinah let herself relax. It was late afternoon, and the falling sun was just beginning to cast a hazy golden glow on the valley.

After a few minutes of consideration, she decided to walk the length of the valley to the orchard. She still had an hour or so before the sun set in the east. She longed to see what rested behind the highest mountain ridge, the northernmost hill with the winding staircase carved deep into its side. Dinah took her time getting there, and found herself wandering along the outer mountain face of the valley. Dim lights from white torches flickered within the fabric tents as the Yurkei settled in, giving the valley an enchanted, mythical glow, like ethereal clouds had floated into its midst.

As she walked, Dinah saw the lowered eyes of the tribe as she passed them, a sign of disrespect. The Yurkei's distrust and anger toward her remained, but she was no longer spit upon or had rocks thrown at her when she left her tent, and that was a vast improvement. Many of them crossed the valley to avoid walking next to her, and Dinah wondered if it was simple hatred, or if they were afraid of her. Her sessions with Bah-kan and Sir Gorrann were growing in popularity, and while she always lost, she was a strong fighter.

Her head spinning with possibilities, Dinah watched a pale mare run feverish loops across the valley. In the distance, dozens of white cranes folded their wings in a massive twig nest that nestled against a rocky outcrop. *I could stay here*, thought Dinah with surprise, *I could be happy here.* She could become a Yurkei warrior, live in a flat tent that was suspended from the mountainside, and learn to love the heights of the ropes strewn between the two mountains.

Yes, she could be happy here, perhaps in time. There was no Wardley, so a truly perfect life was ruled out, but what could she do? He would never find her here, and she would never return to the palace, lest her head grace the white marble slab that had held so many. This valley could hold a possible future for her, and yet her heart kept its distance from the idea. The truth, if she thought about it, was that there was no blissful ending to her story. Her punishment had not been decided, but Morte would be put to death. Her fate awaited his. If she were queen, she certainly would have put the daughter of her most-feared enemy to death. Perhaps Mundoo was having Bah-kan train her so that later it would be a fairer fight to death when her time for execution came. Perhaps to ensure a gloriously bloody death for those who desired justice. Perhaps, but it didn't feel that way.

Her wandering thoughts were interrupted by a delicious smell entering her nostrils. It was a distinct smell, warm and fruity, so unlike the earthy aromas of the Yurkei food. There was a hint of cherry and rose, fresh baked bread and cream. How was that possible? Was she dreaming? She sniffed the air again. *No. The smell is real.* She carefully followed the aroma into a small orchard that sat at the far west end of the valley.

The trees were dense, the swath of fruit trees perhaps a quarter of a mile long. Petite lemon trees dripping with yellow fruit nuzzled up next to lush apple trees, their trunks pushed against floating mulberry trees. Even higher, some fruit trees hovered, connected to the ground by some sort of shiny blue vine that snaked along the path, its purple fruit the size of marbles.

The orchard in itself was marvelous—truly, a wonder—but nothing could compare with what Dinah was smelling: *Home. Tarts. Tea.* In the back of her mind, she knew that she was being led, and yet the smell was everything she missed. Harris and Wardley and warm baths and the palace. *Her palace.* Lights flickered ahead of her in the orchard and she slowed her walk. A nagging voice inside ordered her to draw her dagger, and she obeyed, shielding her eyes from heart-shaped lanterns that seemed to float among the trees. Finally, she emerged from the trees into a small clearing. A long table, magnificently set with towering teacups in every shade and adorned with buckets of flowers, stood before her. The table was covered with all her favorite Wonderland tarts: raspberry and cream, whipped limes and butter roses, deep cocoa mixed with powdered jam. They rested alongside haphazardly piled plates and cups, candles and steaming glasses of hot tea.

A bright pink checkered tablecloth brushed against the tall grass, and in the middle sat a cake. It was a plain white cake with a simple design frosted on the top: a single red heart, sliced from top to bottom. Dinah's own heart clenched, and she clutched her dagger as she began to back away from the table. A light stirred in the trees, and she watched as a tall figure dressed in an elaborate purple robe stepped forward. His long fingers reached out and grasped a cup of tea before pulling it up to his thin lips. He blew on the steam and took a long sip.

"Hello, Your Highness," he said silkily before setting the cup back down. "Won't you have a cup of tea with me? Nothing would make me happier."

Dinah felt the air whoosh out of her chest and saw the orchard spin around her. The man leaned back in his seat and gestured to the table. Cheshire's wicked grin seemed to stretch to the end of the valley. "Cat got your tongue?"

Nine

Dinah was having trouble breathing. Her lungs pressed against her chest, her head pulled against her shoulder—everything, everything was tucking itself into a wild panic. She couldn't quite understand what was happening. There was a table full of food, lights in the trees, and then there was the man responsible for turning her father against her, for helping her father murder her brother and crown Vittiore. Cheshire, the cleverest man in Wonderland. He was right there, his impossibly long body stretched out on a wooden chair, sipping tea like he hadn't a single care in the world. A black goatee had crept across his rubbery face since she had last seen him, and his black hair and eyes glistened with malice in the flickering candlelight. He smiled at her as he took a lavish bite of one of the cocoa tarts, sugar dusting the tip of his brooch, which was adorned with jeweled emblems of the four cards. The symbol that he controlled *all* the Cards.

Dinah noticed the dagger that sat innocently in front of him—his weapon of choice, at the ready if she should attack him. Unmoved by her presence, he licked the tips of his fingers.

"Mmm . . . this one is delicious." His voice jarred Dinah back from the dark paralyzed place in her mind, and her hand brushed the tip of her dagger. His eyes followed her fingers. "I wouldn't throw that, Princess. I believe you seek answers more than you seek revenge, at least at this moment. Trust me when I say I can give you *both*."

Dinah narrowed her eyes and pulled her dagger out of its sheath. Her voice finally clawed its way up her throat. "Tell me one reason why I shouldn't kill you where you sit," she hissed. "Tell me why I shouldn't slit you open right here, and then dine on these tarts as your blood pools over the table. I'd do it happily."

Cheshire's eyes sparkled as he looked through her. "Tarts and blood are not complementary on the palate. Also, it's bad manners, or so your mother should have taught you."

My mother. How dare he? Dinah was on him in a second, grabbing his neck and holding the blade of the dagger against his main artery. She yanked his head back by his greasy black hair. Tarts spilled from their elaborately orchestrated places as his legs slammed against the corner of the table. He twisted suddenly, and Dinah loosened her grip on the dagger, wary of cutting into his thin neck skin. She did want answers—but she also wanted him to feel the fear that could overcome a person in seconds, like diving into icy water. He twisted quickly and furiously, and she pulled back her blade. Soon he was behind her, pressing his body against hers, his hand not on his dagger but wrapped around her mouth. She had made a fatal mistake.

His mouth brushed her ear. "Does this feel familiar, Princess?" he whispered. Then he lowered his voice significantly, and Dinah felt chills rush up her spine. "Perhaps from the night I saved your life and sent you running with a bag strapped across your shoulders? The night when I told you to *go now*, and yet, like an idiot, you visited Charles's chamber instead?" Dinah's body went weak. Cheshire was the stranger who had saved her life? She stopped struggling and stood stunned in the clearing.

Cheshire slowly removed his hand from her mouth and tucked a hair back behind her ear. "Now, Dinah, be a good girl and sit down. I have much to tell you, and you look famished. Have some tarts and tea."

Her body shaking, Dinah let him lead her to a chair at the other end of the table. She still clutched her dagger, and Cheshire made no attempt to take his own—an elaborate show to give the illusion that she was in control, no doubt. At the other end of the table, he settled into his chair and took a sip of tea as he straightened the tablecloth and teacups.

"Now. What kind would you like? Youthberry with lavender? Honeyed Fig? How about a Scarlet Cloud?"

Dinah stared at him, hatred simmering in her eyes.

"That's the one."

Dinah found her voice, more scared than she would have liked it.

"Did you come here to kill me, Cheshire?"

"Oh, no, no. Hmm. Where shall I begin? I have so much to tell you, but I guess we'll start at the very beginning, since most of the things I dabble in start with *me* anyway."

He opened a small porcelain container and began delicately stirring the dry tea leaves inside.

"I was born poor in Verrader, a small fishing village by the Western Slope. I grew up dreaming of the day when I would leave that sorry little town, with its brutal children who would rise up to be nothing more than fishmongers and innkeepers.

"On the day I turned sixteen, I took my father's horse and rode east for Wonderland Palace and the life that I had dreamed of. Upon my arrival, I immediately found work in a jewelry shop. I'm good with numbers, books and things that can be, how shall we say, manipulated? The accountant that had been there before me suddenly fell ill, and I took his place at the shop." He paused. "These are rare tea leaves, brought straight from the palace. All the best for you, my dear."

Using tiny silver tongs, he removed the tea leaves and spread them out on a thin muslin cloth. Dinah kept her eyes on his dagger, her heart thudding against her chest.

Cheshire shook his head. "Anyway, within a year, I became well-known in Wonderland proper for being a man who got what he wanted. I caught the eye of an established banker, who put me in charge of everything when his main account man disappeared. Two years later I was the third-highest-ranking Diamond in the Cards, and I lived a life of counting and calculating. Wonderland Palace had heard word of me and hired me on at the king's bank." Cheshire paused to take a sip of his tea and motioned at the cake in the middle of the table. "Please help yourself." Dinah reached forward slowly, and then with a shove of her hand, pushed the cake off the table into the grass. Cheshire looked exasperated.

"It's not poison, Your Highness, but I won't fault you

for being cautious. You're smart, like me. I mean, gods know people have tried to poison me over the years. Adorable." He took a breath and gave a deceptive smile, his unnaturally white teeth glowing in the darkness.

He folded up the muslin, the tea leaves, and the honeycomb, and crumpled them in his long hands, squeezing and kneading the leaves as they crunched inside. Once he was finished, he siphoned the dust into a tiny metallic cylinder before dropping it into a white porcelain mug, it's handles dotted with cream and pink pearls.

"My dear, I apologize if this next part is hard for you to hear, but it's something you must know. One night, I was invited to attend the ball following the Royal Croquet Game. You know it well. I too share your distaste for such things, but I see them as necessary for social climbing. That night, a radiant young woman was visiting the court. She was from Ierladia, and rumor had it that she was the king's bride to be, the future queen. Her name was Davianna."

Her heart stopped.

"No." Dinah cringed. "No, no."

Cheshire leaned forward, his face sincere. "When I saw

your mother, my world changed. Understand this—all my life I had gathered things for other people—money, goods, revenge. It was my skill. And yet, for the first time, I saw something I wanted for *myself*. She was the most beautiful woman I had ever seen. Her hair was thick and black, like yours, and one could rest a lemon on the curve of her hips. Roses envied the red of her lips. Davianna danced with many men that night—mostly the king—but I waited my turn and took her arm. When she danced with me, both of our worlds seemed to stop. There was an intense connection, a feeling that we had been waiting for each other our entire lives. We fell in love instantly, a thing of fairy tales, but a truth nonetheless. She did not love your father, who was already a brutish man, a drinker, but she married him because she longed to be queen and we both agreed that Wonderland needed a steady hand to rule. I loved your mother for eleven years, with both my soul and body."

He paused and put the cup down, his black eyes staring at her through the shimmering tree lights. "Together we conceived a child and named her Dinah. You, my beautiful and strong daughter."

Dinah gripped a teacup so hard it shattered in her hands. Her mind was having trouble keeping calm, and she heard a cacophony of voices inside her, all in open rebellion, all of them in a state of shock. A drop of blood dripped from her palm onto the table.

Cheshire stared at her for a moment, and began pouring steaming water over the dust.

"*Lies*," she whispered.

Cheshire gave her a sympathetic smile and continued. "Let's not forget that the man you thought was your father tried to kill you, and murdered your brother. You should relish the realization that you do not share his blood. Eventually, the King of Hearts began to suspect your mother of having an affair. There were many times when the king came so close to catching us that I barely escaped in time. In your tenth year of life, Davianna fell ill, very suddenly. I suspected poison, and I still do, though I have never been able to prove who did it." He took a labored breath, and Dinah noticed a slight tremble of his lip. "Imagine, seeing the love of your life dying in front of you and being able to exchange only formal, pleasant words of comfort, your heart feeling like it will burst inside your chest."

From a small jar he grabbed two long black pods and snapped them open. Glistening red cherries spilled out over his fingers.

"I dared not say anything, because who would watch over you if I was executed? The king already suspected that you were not his because of your dark hair and dark eyes—so unlike mad Charles, with his blond hair, surely your father's child. The king was left alone to grieve, but I arranged to have an urgent account matter to discuss with him the very evening of your mother's death. In his drunkenness, he confessed to me that he thought Davianna was unfaithful. I volunteered to root out the culprit, and a month later, with the proof to show, I gave him the head of the Diamond Cards, a handsome young man named Kenrik Ruhalt. Poor Kenrik—he denied it all the way up until your father beheaded him in a secret execution in the dawn hours. I was given his job, and eventually worked my way up until I was the king's chief adviser, the head of the Cards."

Dinah was going to be sick.

"Was it cruel? Yes, but I had to get myself into the best

position to control the king—to make sure that he acted as a steadfast ruler, as it was not his natural inclination. Most important, to keep an eye on you, my daughter."

He dropped the cherries one by one into the mug.

Cheshire smiled and looked down at the table. "I had already interceded where I dared to make sure that you had a good childhood, even before Davianna's death. I arranged for the Ghanes to move into the palace so that you might have a friend in Wardley, since before his arrival you were a lonely, moody child. I convinced the king to hire gentle Harris as your guardian instead of the cruel governess For-sythe, who was the customary teacher for the royal children. I made sure that you were kept safe, as safe as you could be, from the king's rage. I encouraged him to go to war with the Yurkei when you were very young, so that you and your mother could have some peace.

"But, as you know, the man you have called father for so long is a rapacious and obsessive man. He was sure that you were not his child, and was convinced that you could never follow him to the throne because you would soon marry and either banish or execute him. He told me of an idea that he had been thinking of for a long time, the idea that he would create his own heir, the heir he had always wanted. He needed to find a child about the same age as his daughter. A girl, for a boy would be prone to rebellion. What he needed was someone who could be his puppet, someone who he could control without problems arising. As his adviser, I warned him against the idea, but I had long suspected that he would never put you on the throne. I did all I could to keep him away from you, but his rage and paranoid delusions were growing, though he kept them concealed behind an infuriating mask of contempt. I could never risk my position as adviser. So I agreed to help him find his little princess.

"The king told his council that he was going off on a hunt, but instead we rode hard for the outer villages on the lower Western Slope—isolated sea towns where we would go unnoticed. On our way there, we chanced upon a small hut, far outside of any town or village. A woman and a girl were making necklaces out of seashells. The girl was breathtakingly beautiful, ethereal almost, and most important, she had yellow hair the exact same color as the king's. That night the king burned a small heart on to her back to remind her who he was, and rode homeward with her strapped to Morte's back. A few Cards followed behind with her mother, Faina Baker, and threw her in the Black Towers upon their arrival to Wonderland proper. The girl was christened Vittiore—a noble name—and put in front of the court as his long-lost daughter.

"That day I realized your life was even more in danger than I had previously thought, and that the closer you got to your coronation, the more the king would try to get rid of you—either that or try to persuade you to give up your rightful throne. That would never work. Even as a child, you longed to be queen."

He grinned as he began stirring the tea. Steam curled out of the cup, a dark red.

"Your thirst for power matches my own. I showed you the tunnels that afternoon, for it was all I could do at that moment to help you. Someday, I thought to myself, you would have need of them. I started trying to clue you in to the king's motivations, to the fact that a vast conspiracy to crown Vittiore was growing around you, one that I was a part of—but I undermined it whenever I could. The king made his stance known during the Royal Croquet Game, and I knew it wasn't long before he would try to have you murdered or exiled. I passed you a note at the dinner that evening, in a small bottle. It might seem coy, but I wanted you to figure it out on your own. After all, I knew my daughter to be intelligent and curious, just like me."

Dinah's throat was dry and stinging, her eyes filled with tears. *This couldn't be true. It couldn't be.*

"I shouldn't have worried. Using the tunnels, you made your way to the Black Towers and discovered the truth about Vittiore, even if you didn't put it together right away, for by then Faina Baker had gone mad. The king was hungry for a shift in power, and once he learned of your excursion to the Black Towers, he decided to behead Faina. It was a message for you, but its true purpose was to remind Vittiore of what would happen if she ever rebelled against him. It was unthinkably cruel, but it was a well-instructed lesson to both of you to stay out of his way.

"By then a sort of madness had overtaken the king, and he began muttering dark, violent things. I worried for your safety. I pressed the king to reveal his plans to me, but he refused. Even his most trusted advisers remained in the dark."

Dinah's hands were gripping the tablecloth, her nails tearing through the thin fabric. Her world was collapsing, inside and outside. Her watery eyes made the stars look like they were falling. She stopped breathing. She stared at Cheshire as he continued, but all she saw was Charles.

Cheshire blew on the steaming mug.

"On the night of your brother's murder, I was out meeting with some colleagues who lived in the court just outside the palace—Lords Delmont and Sander, I'm sure you know them."

Dinah nodded impatiently.

"I returned late, much past the midnight hour. The king burst into my chamber, unannounced and covered with blood. He was hysterical. I calmed him down but could not hide my horror when he told me that he had just thrown Charles from a window and murdered Lucy and Quintrell. He said that he was going to frame you, so that you might never ascend to the throne. Instead, it would be off with your head, or you would be thrown into the Black Towers for the remainder of your life. As he rocked himself by the window, muttering of justice and how your mother's bastard would be tried for her crimes, I knew that every moment of my life had boiled down to this one. How could I help save my daughter without revealing the truth to the king?

"I told the king to change, bathe, and gather his Cards to help apprehend you. I ran—how I ran—first to the kitchens and then to the weapons room. I knew you would never survive without food in the wild. You were raised in a palace that gave you everything you ever needed. After I packed your bag, I ran to your room, where I knocked Harris and Emily unconscious. For a few seconds, I watched you sleeping—my daughter, the pride of my heart, with a face like her mother's and a fierce intelligence not unlike my own. I had never seen you so close, so perfect, the blood of my veins sleeping before me. I vowed I would do whatever it took to help you survive. Then you awoke . . . and tried to kill me."

He gave a chuckle, and Dinah remembered the horror of waking up to the dark shrouded figure in her room.

Cheshire took a sip of the tea. "Ah, perfect. A lovely Scarlet Cloud.

"Though you did not follow my *exact* directions, you did escape, and in what *grand* fashion! You left behind a bloody mess, you stole your father's Hornhoov and then outran him and his army in a chase that the peasants will be talking about a hundred years from now!" He clapped his hands with glee. "I couldn't have planned it better myself. After you left, the king quickly declared you a traitor to the realm and placed the crown on Vittiore's head. The coronation was the biggest that Wonderland had ever seen, and I believe she was glad to receive the crown. The king left immediately after to resume the hunt for you, and it was the opportunity I had been waiting for. A chance to find you, to make sure that you were surviving in the Twisted Wood.

"Whispered sources told me of a Spade tracker that had a long-standing grudge against the king, and I sought him out. I made a deal with your Sir Gorrann. He would track you down—with the king in tow—but would find you beforehand and take you deep into the Yurkei Mountains, where you would be safe from the king. He tracked you a little too fast but as you can see, he kept you safe, fed, and began training you to fight."

Cheshire rubbed the front of his neck where Dinah had poked him with the dagger. A smile played across his face. "I joined the king on this mission to hunt you down, and as soon as I knew that you were safely in Sir Gorrann's care, I quietly took my leave from the king's side and followed an alternate path up to Hu-Yuhar, but not before I convinced him to abandon his chase and return to Wonderland Palace." He absentmindedly fingered his sparkling brooch.

"I saw you in the darkness that night, standing still in the black dress I had packed for you. I was proud that you had used it so well, and so furious that you would put yourself at that much risk, all for a chance at revenge. Please forgive me for my delay." He gestured to the elaborate table. "One would not call me a light packer. But, finally, here we are, father and daughter, reunited at last, without secrets or lies between us. *I have longed for this moment.*

"Tea, my daughter?"

He handed the cup to her. Dinah took it with trembling fingers.

Dinah's voice caught in her throat. She wanted to throw herself at him, to take his life, to beat him, to embrace him, to weep and laugh, all at once. She felt nauseated and dizzy, confused and elated. *It was too much.* She could barely strangle out a single bitter sentence as she set the cup down. "Why are you here?"

His fingers stopped moving against his cup and he cautiously stood and walked slowly over to Dinah. Kneeling before her, he bowed his jet-black head in the moonlight and then looked up at her, his white smile stretching wide over his thin face.

"*Why?* Because you are my daughter, the pride and purpose of my life, and I have come to aid you as you reclaim the throne in Wonderland. *Why?* Because you are the true heir of Queen Davianna, and your claim to the throne is stronger than Vittiore's, who is a pauper, related to no one. I will help you take your vengeance against the king, with a mighty army of the Yurkei behind you. *Why?* Because you were born to wear the crown, and I will not see Davianna's daughter slowly waste away in the Yurkei Mountains. Dinah, you must conquer."

Without warning, he pressed his lips to her hand, and Dinah felt a wave of revulsion wash over her. She yanked her hand back as if she had been burned. Tea sloshed over the table.

Cheshire stood and walked to the end of the table, where he gently picked up a covered silver cake platter. He set it in front of Dinah's chair. "A gift for my daughter."

"I don't want to see it."

"You must."

Shaking, Dinah lifted the lid. Underneath it was her princess crown—the gold and ruby crown, a ring of hearts that blazed like fire. The crown she had left behind. Cheshire picked up the crown and lowered it onto her head. She had forgotten how solid it was, how its points dug into her skull, and the flush of happiness she felt when it rested heavily on her temples. The lanterns in the trees flickered, and she heard the rustling of a crane's wings overhead. She looked down at Cheshire, now kneeling in front of her. His black eyes met hers, a mirror image. Her enemy, her father?

His voice boomed through the trees. "Rise, Dinah, and become the Queen of Hearts. It is time to embrace your fate."

The night held its breath. Dinah looked at him, his black eyes glittering in the starlight. The Scarlet Cloud rose out of her teacup, blurring her vision red.

Embrace your fate.

She ran.

Ten

The once Princess of Wonderland crashed through the brush. Twigs and branches broke as she plunged through the Yurkei orchard, far away from Cheshire, far away from everything he had said. Her breath was loud and jagged, full of pain and confusion.

Sharp branches ripped at her arms and legs, their thorns piercing her soft flesh as she rushed past. The dark branches arched their spindly arms overhead as Dinah escaped deeper into the orchard. There were strange blue lights flickering in the trees, but then again, what wasn't strange in Wonderland?

Something large sailed over her head, and Dinah heard the cry of a crane as she raced through a bramble bush, her legs moving faster than she had ever known they could.

It didn't take long for her to come to the end of the orchard, and when she emerged from the trees, she was surprised to see a sheer cliff face rising up before her, looking like bone in the white moonlight. Dinah buried her face in her hands as she gradually remembered where she was: the Yurkei valley, surrounded by mountains. There was nowhere else to go but up. She looked around for a few minutes before spotting the winding path that Sir Gorrann had mentioned in passing. It was steep, looping over on itself as it snaked its way up the mountain, narrow and well-worn. Dinah found herself running up the path without consideration. She just needed to flee, to anywhere, to anything. It was all too much. The path climbed higher into the sky, until Dinah was surrounded by a thick white mist that clouded her vision. She pressed her back against the wall and continued her crablike climb until the ghostly mist gave way to cool air.

Dinah was out of breath when she reached the top of the cliff face. She swayed on her feet and was surprised to find herself toeing the line of consciousness. The healed wound on her shoulder ached and pulsed with each frayed inhale, and Dinah found herself heaving onto the pebbly ground. She rested her head on the cool stone for a few minutes, focusing on breathing normally again. Wiping her mouth, she pushed off her knees and looked around.

She was truly alone. The ground before her was flat and made of stone—a circular platform carved from the mountain that dropped into air on each side. Small etchings had been carved into the ground, tiny little marks that told an ancient story of sacrifice and redemption. They were the religious markings of the Yurkei tribe. She ran her fingers lightly over them. Harris would have loved to see this. He found the Yurkei religion fascinating. Dinah lifted her eyes and looked out past the edge of the stone circle. She could see the entire Yurkei valley if she stood on one side; the floating white tents attached to the side of the mountain, each of them emitting a dim glow. The great stone birds stood erect and silent with Mundoo's tent suspended between them. The flowing creek behind the tents gurgled contentedly. It was a quiet night in Hu-Yuhar, and the only noises came from the herds of wild horses playing below, their happy whinnies soothing to her ears.

Dinah let her eyes wander to the northernmost part of the valley, and they rested upon the subtly lit orchard where Cheshire had waited for her, his long hands clasping a teacup. He was still there, no doubt biding his time before he could crush everything she knew into a fine powder, like the sugar that dusted his brooch. *Cheshire, her father?* Dinah pressed her hands against the unyielding stone. *Could this be true? And if it was?* Should she be grateful that her own father did not try to kill her but rather saved her life? Or should she be furious that her entire life was a well-orchestrated lie? The truth had been kept from her, not only by Cheshire but by her own mother, the only person who truly loved her. Her mother, Davianna, who had loved Cheshire and betrayed the king. Dinah imagined her mother's soft hands wrapped around Cheshire's neck as they danced in the Great Hall, those same hands that had always caressed Dinah's face so lovingly. . . . Dinah shook her head to clear the image. Was this just another of Cheshire's games? It was possible, but there was an unmistakable thrumming in her heart that told her it was not.

Part of her wished that she had slit his throat before he could speak. *Or did she?* Dinah didn't know what she wanted. Her emotions whirled, a churning storm inside her. Was she to become a grateful, doting daughter? The warrior he had been training her to become? An exiled princess, a Yurkei prisoner? Was she full of rage like the man she believed to be her father, or full of grace like Charles, her *half* brother? If she was not the daughter of the King of Hearts but the daughter of Cheshire, a traitor—what was she now? Who was she now?

"Who would you have me be?" she angrily called to the stars, tonight all circling around one singular bright star that lingered lazily over the mountains. Her voice rose to a strained yell, choked with emotion. "I *said*, who would you have me *be*?"

"I think yeh know," answered a familiar voice.

Dinah didn't bother to turn around. "How did you find me?" she sniffed.

He gave a gruff laugh. "I'm a tracker, remember? It wasn't exactly hard—there was nowhere else for yeh to go but up. Yer in a damn valley." She lowered her eyes, refusing to look at him. "You best not go any farther though, lest Mundoo think you are trying to escape."

She spun around to face him. "You work for Cheshire. You betrayed me. You lied to me."

Sir Gorrann walked up beside her, and Dinah heard the crunch of his heavy boots echoing over the cavernous drop. "I never lied to yeh. Yeh never really asked about Cheshire. Did he hire me to find yeh? Indeed. And did I? Yes. I saved yer life, girl, and I would save it again. When Cheshire came to me, he dangled a promise: if I was to find yeh, I would get to see for myself that the king was brought to justice, hopefully by yer hand. Not only that, but I would see him stripped of all power and pride. That is what I long for—for him to suffer as I have suffered. Only his wayward daughter could give it to me."

He paused and scratched at his beard as he stared at Dinah, framed by the bright stars. "Though it pains me to tell yeh . . . truth be told, after a while, things changed.

Dinah, I've grown a bit fond of yeh, and I'll fight beside yeh, whatever yeh decide." He looked gently into her eyes, his face etched with the love of a father.

"Yeh remind me of my Ioney, if she had been given the chance to live. Yer fierce and strong, full of rash emotion. Hear me that my loyalty is to yeh, and yeh alone. If yeh ask me to kill him"—he gestured his head toward the orchard below, to Cheshire—"I will. Though, keep in mind, he might get me first. Cheshire is already four steps ahead of wherever you think you are. Listen to me, girl: don't ever underestimate that man. And don't blindly trust him either."

Sir Gorrann paused before shivering once. "If we're going to be chattin' awhile, I'm building a fire. It's cold as a proper lady's bed up here."

Dinah pulled her knees into her chest and shivered as she stared at the whitewashed valley that stretched out toward the east. "That man—you mean my father?" Sir Gorrann did not reply but instead made quick work building a small fire against the night chill from a dried bird's nest. His skill was enviable, and soon warm flames crackled and hissed as they sat together in silence.

Finally, Dinah spoke, her voice breaking with emotional exhaustion. "What does he want me to do?"

Sir Gorrann shifted on the ground and withdrew a pipe. "Isn't it obvious? He wants yeh to take what's yers. Yer mother's throne at Wonderland Palace. He wants yeh to rule."

"And what do you want?"

Sir Gorrann blew a stream of smoke into the air, the tail end smelling of horses and sweet leaves. "I want yeh to do what yeh believe is right. I long for the king to be brought to justice, but I'll bring him to justice one way or another, now or twenty years from now, either at yer side or by some other means. I'll not make yeh carry my burden."

Dinah frowned. "Justice." She laughed wildly. "Do I not long for that as well? The king killed my brother. Cheshire saved my life."

"That he did. And from the sounds of it, more than once. But yeh don't owe him anything. Yeh do not want to owe a man like that. Do yeh understand? Yeh don't." The Spade's voice was rising. Dinah shushed him with a glance. He took a breath. "Sorry. Do yeh believe him? About him being yer father?"

Dinah shut her eyes. *That was the question, wasn't it?* She didn't want to believe him. She wanted everything to go back to how it was long before—when she was a child in her mother's arms, when Charles was still alive, when the King of Hearts was still her father and she could look on him with pride, even when she trembled in fear at his fury. Back to a time when Wardley was near, an apple in one hand and reins in another. Dinah considered carefully before she spoke.

"I don't want to believe him, and yet, when he said those . . . *things*, I could feel that pieces of my life that were scattered about were clicking into place, like a key in a lock. Everything fits together now, in a way it didn't before." She shook her head. "It makes sense—why I don't look anything like my father—er, the king—or Charles. Why the king hated me my entire life, why he beat my mother, why he so frequently escaped to go to war. Why he never wanted me to share his throne." She let out a low scream before beating one clenched fist against her chest. "Gods, I am such a *fool*!"

No sooner had her voice echoed over the rocks than a loud clamor of high screams echoed back. Both Dinah and Sir Gorrann froze in place. The screams grew louder, until Dinah realized that what she was hearing was a growing cacophony of high-pitched birdcalls. Crawling on her hands and knees, Dinah cautiously peeked over the edge of the stone circle and immediately felt her stomach drop. What she had guessed to be nothing but whitewashed stone of the valley were actually birds, hundreds of thousands of white cranes nesting fifty feet below the edge of the cliff. Their rising sound was deafening, and Dinah felt her pulse quicken. The birds could kill them both. With newfound understanding, she glanced back at the religious markings on the ground, the dark brown spots that stained the stone in certain places. She closed her eyes and saw a prisoner, tied down to the stone, left for the birds. *Oh gods.*

Sir Gorrann looked over the edge with a grimace. "We shouldn't stay here long."

Dinah watched the cranes in silence, her black eyes wide with fascination. The birds eventually calmed down, their wings tucking back, settling into their one massive nest. Dinah thought she spotted the body of a horse. It was still moving slightly. Their cries faded, and Dinah spoke quietly.

"Cheshire wants me to reclaim my throne. He thinks I am a conqueror. A conqueror without an army."

"The Yurkei will fight for you."

"Fight for me?" She laughed out loud. "They *hate* me. Have you seen their faces when I walk by?" She saw them then, their glowing blue eyes following her every move, their brows knotted in fury. "The Yurkei will fight for Mundoo. Besides, there aren't very many of them, not compared to the Cards."

"Have you ever seen the Yurkei fight?" replied Sir Gorrann. "One Yurkei can best four Cards." He shook his head. "They move with a certain swiftness. It's unnerving."

"It's still not enough," she corrected him. "If it did happen, which I'm not saying it will, how would it . . . work?"

Sir Gorrann took his time phrasing his careful reply, one eye trained on the simmering crane nest below. "Cheshire has been meeting with Mundoo for a few days now."

Dinah bit her lip. *So that's where Mundoo had been going.*

"They are still hammering out an acceptable treaty. From what I can gather, in return for fighting for yeh, they will get all their lands back, and probably much more."

Dinah shook her head in amazement. "What are we talking about? Just a few hours ago, I was a prisoner of the Yurkei, and a few weeks before that, an outlaw, and before that a princess!"

Sir Gorrann shook his head. "Yeh never were just a prisoner."

"Maybe I just want to be a prisoner! Or a nobody! Maybe I just want to stay here and live a normal life. Have you considered that?"

Sir Gorrann's golden eyes studied her face. "Yeh don't want that. I know yeh."

Dinah felt a blush rise up her cheeks. "It doesn't matter. What you're telling me is that I'm to lead an army to Wonderland Palace that may be defeated? Am I correct? You're saying that I should lead this endeavor in a doomed attempt to sit on a throne because my mother once sat there?" Her voice was growing ever louder, more and more agitated. She felt the fury rising in her chest, the black boiling. She leaped to her feet. "Look at me and tell me—who am I, Sir Gorrann? Who do you see when you look at me? Do you see my father's daughter? Do you see Cheshire? Do you see a whimpering girl or a Yurkei warrior? A spoiled princess? A conqueror? And who are you? A lonely man? Do you hope for a crown upon your head, Sir Gorrann?"

She was yelling now, and she could hear the squawks from below as the birds began to stir once again.

"Be quiet! Do yeh long to be pecked to death?" Sir Gorrann was growing livid. His face was contorted with an anger that seemed to light up the valley. "Yer acting like a child, that's what yeh are! A spoiled brat who has been given everything! And now, a man brings an army to yer feet and yeh aren't sure what to do? That's not for me to tell yeh. I'm just a dirty Spade, a tracker, a broken man. I know yeh see that."

They were furious with each other now, yelling in whispers, their sentences overlapping, spit flying from their mouths. Sir Gorrann's forehead pulsed with a purple vein. "Who am I, yeh ask? I am not who I once was, a man with a wife and a daughter. We become who we must to overcome pain and to make things right again. Everything I have done, I have done to get justice for my family. I have not brought yeh this far to ask someone else what yeh should do!"

Sir Gorrann pointed to one of the vertical rock faces that divided the west and east sides of the valley. His small fire had thrown its light, and their large shadows danced across it. "I know who I see. No matter what Cheshire said, yer still the same person that yeh were before yeh came upon that tea table. It's not his arrival that has changed anything; it's just yer understanding of the past. There's nothing I can tell yeh, but I would say to look with yer own damn eyes!" He began walking toward the sloping path that led down to the valley.

"Go ahead and leave," she said quietly. "I don't want to see anyone right now." The black fury was raging inside of her. She would not let his arguments push her over the edge of sanity.

With a huff, he began descending down the winding path, muttering to himself about "Cheshire's mad daughter." Dinah was suddenly alone, comforted only by the crackling fire that continued to project massive dancing shadows on the rock walls. She felt swept away by a surge of emotion, as if she was drowning in a tidal wave of her own confusion.

A thousand different hands were reaching inside her head, each yanking at a string. Her onetime father, the King of Hearts. Her now father, Cheshire, with his slippery feline smile. Sir Gorrann. Mundoo. Bah-kan. Wardley, Charles, Harris, Faina Baker, Vittiore. Their faces ran together, each one a part of her but none of them giving her the answer she needed. Images chased one another through her mind, a game of insane tag: Wardley, kissing her under the Julla Tree. Her mother, looking at her reflection in the mirror. Charles, a finely crafted hat in his hand. Lucy and Quintrell, bloody and piled in a closet. She closed her eyes and felt the heat from the fire sear close to her face. She willed the thousand voices to be quiet.

Unconsciously, she raised her arms, the pain of her shoulder making her wince through the confusion. *Be silent*, she shouted to the voices in her head. *Be silent!* she commanded again. Finally, she pushed them down until it was only her own voice that she heard. She lowered her hands. There was a stillness within her, and Dinah allowed herself to reach inside to gather her thoughts. When she opened her eyes again, she looked up at the rocky cliff face and immediately saw what Sir Gorrann had been pointing at. Stunned, Dinah lifted her chin in a way that she hadn't done since she fled the palace. With the fire leaping behind her, the shadow of her figure loomed huge on the rock walls. On her head sat the shadow of the crown that Cheshire had placed upon her.

Dinah reached up and felt the rim of the crown with her shaking fingers, the gold warm from the growing flames. She had forgotten she was wearing it, she was so used to its weight and feel. It was natural for her—she had been practically born wearing that crown. It stayed put even as she had torn through the trees and bramble. It felt *right* on her head, and the spikes that dug into her temple gave her a steadiness that she hadn't felt in a long time. She stared at her shadow, and the commanding figure with the crown shimmered in the flames. Her mind cleared. The answer was here. *This was who she was, who she had always been.* She was no one's daughter, no one's warrior, no one's scapegoat or prisoner. She wasn't a spoiled princess or the savior of a foreign people. Dinah raised her eyes to the circling stars, and her shadow straightened in accordance.

I am the queen, she thought.

I am the Queen of Hearts, born to sit on one of two Heart thrones. I am the Queen of Wonderland and I will have the crown that my brother made for me. I will take it with fury and swords and whatever help I can find. Pride blossomed in her chest, and every inch of her skin felt alive with promise and purpose. Suddenly aware of everything touching her, pressing against her skin, clinging to her neck, Dinah began taking off her clothing. She flung down her dagger and pulled the red tunic that represented Wonderland over her head. Off came the feathery Yurkei pants and the boots that had been tucked into her bag, a million years ago. When she was finished, Dinah was without chains to bind or gifts to bribe or tools to shame her. She was naked, with only the crown on her head, a crown that was her right by birth, by the line of her mother. *I am the queen.* Everyone in Wonderland would bow before her. She wasn't afraid, not anymore. *I am the queen.*

Alive in every way, Dinah flung a large burning piece of wood over the edge of the cliff, where it landed with a fiery burst in the massive nest. The air instantly thrummed with the sound of a thousand wings, and Dinah watched without fear as the sky filled with enormous white cranes. They rushed at her with beating wings and sharp beaks, but she stood firm, naked and flushed, with only the crown on her head. They circled her, their loud cries coming ever closer, their beaks brushing her skin. "Go!" she screamed. "GO!" All around her was a sea of white feathers, but Dinah dared not close her eyes. There was a moment when the seething flock hovered just above her and all around her, an angry hissing and squawking swarm, considering an attack on this strange creature wearing a crown and blazing with righteous anger. Dinah's black eyes stared at the birds, unflinching, daring them to touch her. The birds seemed to pause, violence on their minds, then, at the last moment, they rose into the air in an ever-widening spiral, blocking out the stars. She had faced down the gods and won.

I am the Queen of Hearts, she thought, *and I will take my throne.*

Once the birds had completely disappeared into the night sky, she breathed deeply until her heart stopped pounding. Dinah left the fire to burn itself out, but not before she glanced once more at her imposing shadow, so ferocious and secure, with the pointed tips of her crown brushing the top of the cliff face. A nagging voice told her that while she wasn't as mighty as *that* queen, she would have to try to be. No matter the fear that would inevitably get in her way, she had to try.

Dinah begrudgingly pulled all her clothing back on and gave one quick glance at the Hu-Yuhar valley below. A crowd of Yurkei was gathering, and their voices gave way to silent awe as she walked down the steep path carved into the rock wall. A nervous group of men waited for her at the bottom of the narrow staircase: Cheshire, his purple robes billowing in the wind and his hands resting together as if in prayer; Sir Gorrann, his weathered face a mask of concern; Mundoo, fierce and proud, the leader of his people; and Bah-kan, who towered over all of them, terrifying and vicious, clutching his Heartsword. The men watched her as she made her way down, her emotionless face betraying nothing. She drew ever closer to the small group of men who had played her like a pawn, those men who had deftly moved her toward her destiny. Cheshire's face broke into a wide smile when he saw the crown on her head. He quickly bent at the knee and bowed before her in grand fashion. Sir Gorrann followed. Mundoo and Bah-kan simply nodded in her direction. They would not bow before her.

Mundoo cleared his mighty throat. "Princess. We have much to speak about."

Dinah wouldn't realize until later that three simple words would forever change the face of Wonderland.

"It's Your Highness," she corrected him. "And I imagine we do."

Eleven

Seasons changed the landscape with alarming ferocity as the next few months flew by. Dinah and her army marched south. *Even the grass is different here in the Darklands*, thought Dinah as she watched the pale blue ferns ripple across the murky landscape. Everything was softer and wetter. Her steed pawed impatiently at the ground, thirsty and ready to plunge his head into the swirling currents of cool water that ran just beneath the moss. Her hair, damp and twisted with white ribbons, blew out before her. Dinah shuddered in the morning air as something round and glowing slithered just underneath the foamy brush. She had expected the South to be warm and humid. She had been right about the humidity, but with the moist air of the Darklands came a certain chill in the early morning, the wet air holding on to the bite of night.

It had been a hellish march. They had lost several Yurkei along the way, between the hidden bogs and the strange poisonous creatures that seemed to lurk under every rock. Disturbingly, the Twisted Wood seemed downright tame compared to the Darklands. As she dug her hand into her steed's tangled mane, Dinah hummed a song softly under her breath, a song her mother had taught her so very long ago. A song, she now knew, Davianna had learned from Cheshire.

The landscape was brutal, but even with danger surrounding her on all sides, Dinah felt stronger than ever. Her crown rested on top of her head, its rightful place, and Dinah felt powerful in the high saddle. Her stomach grumbled loudly. She was hungry, as she had been ever since they started their march southward. Moving a small army required much food, and there was never enough, it seemed, to satisfy. Everyone could eat at least five times more—even the future queen, who slept in a battered tent, curled around her sword. Dinah was still humming when Sir Gorrann trotted up next to her on Cyndy.

"Sir Gorrann, good morning."

He didn't waste time with pleasantries. "Yer Highness, there is a conflict between two of the warriors. Ju-Kule and Freyuk are about to come to blows. Yeh must come quickly— their quarrel will surely end in even more divided loyalty among the Yurkei."

Dinah nodded her head and with a click of her tongue sent her steed galloping toward the camp—a small city of circular white tents that held a thousand Yurkei warriors and, so far, about three hundred rogue Cards. *Wonderful*, she thought. *Another problem, another small battle.* Preparing for a war, it turned out, was very complicated and took months. She bit her cheek nervously as she thought back on all the conflicts that had followed her down from the mountains.

The night she had accepted her fate as queen, she had, along with Sir Gorrann and Cheshire, climbed up into Mun-doo's tent. The fear had returned when she stared up at the ladder, but this time she had something other than survival at hand—she had reasons to live: vengeance and the throne. As the ladder billowed out behind her, Dinah forced herself to climb. *I am the queen.* Almost immediately after they began their tense discussion, it was very clear that each member of the war council entered with their own agenda. Mundoo longed for his people's complete autonomy and independence from Wonderland Palace. In return for his people's support in battle, he demanded the release of all their former lands back to the Yurkei, all the way north from the Ninth Sea up through the Todren and to the east, from the Twisted Wood until the end of the Yurkei Mountains. He also decreed that a representative of the Yurkei people was to sit on the queen's council, once established, and would have a vote in Wonderland's affairs that both did and did not concern the Yurkei. It was a steep price to pay for her army, one that she would surely feel later if she was indeed crowned queen. Part of the Yurkei lands included Ierladia, her mother's hometown, the northern Wonderland stronghold. The negotiations over Ierladia had taken three days, but in the end, a compromise had been reached. Mundoo agreed that the citizens and buildings of Ierladia would remain unharmed under Yurkei rule. While the Yurkei would ultimately own the city, Ierladia would still function as it always had—by doing trade and commerce with Wonderland Palace. The Yurkei would then reap a hefty portion of their taxes as the owners of the city. Tax was a strange concept to the Yurkei, but eventually they acceded to Cheshire's plan.

Dinah's newfound father came with his own set of demands: he would take his seat as the queen's main adviser, the head of her council, and he would remain in charge of all the Cards, as well as the acting Diamond Card in charge of the treasury. His powers would increase to include a seat on the Yurkei council. Without expressly saying so, Cheshire made sure that he would be the most powerful person in the palace aside from the queen. Bahkan wanted lands within Yurkei territory and a royal pardon for his desertion from the Cards, and he would have it, but only if he agreed to be Dinah's personal bodyguard until she was crowned. Sir Gorrann said that he would negotiate with Dinah alone, but so far he had remained silent and impassive, wanting nothing apparently.

After the negotiations were signed and sealed, four swift

horses bearing Yurkei riders were sent to store the documents in the four corners of Wonderland, so that there might always be one treaty that remained safe, even if the rest were destroyed. After the documents were carried away, Dinah nervously prepared for the ancient Yurkei sealing ritual. Wearing little more than a few feathers, Dinah stood perfectly still for hours as the words of the treaty were painted on her body with white paint by silent Yurkei women. The words trailed down from her eyes in straight lines to the edge of her toes, and by the end, there wasn't an inch of her skin unmarked with white paint. The words of their treaty trailed from her cheeks, her belly, her fingertips. Mundoo had the same treaty inscribed down his body, and when they were done, both Dinah and Mundoo were led into a ringed circle of fire, a subdued crane tied to each of their wrists. The Yurkei rose in song, an unnerving wail that resonated through the narrow valley.

For hours they sang, Dinah and Mundoo standing perfectly still until their legs trembled beneath them. Finally, at the excited shout of the crowd, the two of them neared each other as the stars swirled above. When they were close enough to touch, the cranes leaped from their wrists and flapped toward each other. Mundoo and Dinah were yanked together, the strings holding their cranes twisting and tangling while the birds fluttered and fought. The words written on their bodies smeared together, the melting paint mixing with their sweat as they struggled to back away from each other. Finally, a Yurkei priestess gave a shout and they both released their birds into the sky. The words were now one, blended forever, absorbed into their skin. Dinah's black eyes met Mundoo's shimmering blue irises as they stood silently, surrounded by the roaring fire. What she had seen in them both reassured and frightened Dinah. Mundoo was resilient, and she saw a passion to rule blazing in his eyes that was not unlike her own. *She was a queen and he was a chief.* They were the same. A pact had been made, a promise sealed. Dinah had never felt more alive and gave a shout to the sky, her head thrown back in glory.

After she had cleaned up, she joined the Yurkei for a celebratory feast alongside Bah-kan, Sir Gorrann, and her two Yurkei guards. It was a meal to put all others to shame, even the endless food she had known at Wonderland Palace.

Birds of every type were paraded in on the backs of Yurkei warriors. Each bite tingled with rich spices, woodsy and full of flavor, each taste manipulated by Iu-Hora, their witch doctor. Dinah was given piles of edible mushrooms, each one producing a unique effect—some made her melancholy, while others made her silly. Some produced a feeling of intense passion that climaxed in seconds and left her breathless, clutching the table. One gave her a hallucination of the palace, filled with thumping red hearts and fluttering peacocks. Another showed her a river of blood, soaking her feet. The effects weren't lasting—most were no more than a minute—so Dinah eagerly awaited what each new mushroom would bring.

Cheshire sat beside her on one side and Sir Gorrann on the other; and while Cheshire was constantly trying to engage her with compliments or observations, she couldn't bring herself to be kind to him, not yet. She did find herself staring at him when he wasn't looking, taking in his jet-black hair and eyes, so like her own. She imagined him with her mother, laughing and touching, finding every spare moment to be together, caught up in the danger of their forbidden passion. At times the idea made her sick. Since he had arrived, Cheshire had given her a number of gifts—a lovely diamond brooch in the shape of a cat, a heavy purple riding cloak, a new set of dark red leather boots imprinted with a heart on each heel. She pulled on the boots immediately and shoved the other presents into her bag. He could not buy her loyalty or love, not yet, but she needed new boots and so allowed herself to slip into their rich soles, her sore feet rejoicing.

Her training with Bah-kan and Sir Gorrann continued—brutal mornings, every day—until she was able to spar competently with Sir Gorrann, even beating him on occasion. All the mornings she had played swords with Wardley were returning to her, and her strokes became quick and hard as her body intuitively spun and leaped. Somehow, without her noticing, the blade and her body had become one. One morning, as Dinah was eating, Cheshire approached and invited her to train with him on throwing daggers. Dinah reluctantly agreed, but to her dismay found that she thoroughly enjoyed herself. There was something about winging a dagger at a tree that released her grow-ing anxiety about leading an army. Cheshire was extremely skilled with a dagger, and Dinah realized that he had generously allowed her to hold her dagger to his throat in the orchard that evening. He could have disarmed or killed her at any time.

As they threw the knives, Cheshire recounted for her parts of her childhood that she had almost forgotten—her fifth birthday, a certain croquet game, when she broke her leg climbing a statue. He had indeed been watching her, but she told herself that it meant nothing. It was hard enough to consider that she was of his blood, let alone to develop the daughter–father bond that she had been lacking her entire life. And so she didn't speak. She just flung the daggers, loving the *thwunk!* against the tree bark when the knife made contact.

It was decided that Dinah would take a thousand Yurkei warriors with her as she marched south. If there was to be even the slightest hope of victory against the king's army of ten thousand Cards and growing, then they needed the support of the rogue Cards who dwelled inside the Darklands. These were men, dangerous men, who had deserted the Cards and fled south, where they could live in relative freedom outside Wonderland law. Then again, they had to live in the Darklands, which to Dinah seemed to be punishment enough.

Mundoo and his army of four thousand Yurkei would march north, gathering men from the smaller tribes that lay scattered below the Todren, and make their way down from there to Wonderland Palace. Not only would this ensure that the palace would be attacked from both the north and the south—essential when the palace was surrounded by a circular wall—but the King of Hearts would surely focus on Mundoo's large and noisy army, allowing Dinah and her small army to creep up from behind. Cheshire's hope was that Dinah's army would surprise him, or at least alarm the Cards. They would attack the palace together, independent armies working as one. He was unnervingly clever in battle strategy, and Dinah saw instantly why the king had chosen him over his peers to be his adviser. Cheshire's mind was not unlike his dagger. Razor sharp and lethal, it could be wielded adeptly in whatever way he chose. He explained that her small army of Yurkei would be there for her protection in the Darklands, but they also served as a symbol to the rogue Cards of her commitment to a new kind of existence, one in which Wonderlanders, Cards, and Yurkei all existed and fought together to end tyranny. In his words, seeing the Queen of Hearts leading an army of Yurkei warriors would be enough to sway even the hardest mind. "Wars," he reminded her, "are won in the mind, not on the field."

On the day before their departure, a few months' time since Dinah had descended from the mountain with her crown, the women of the Yurkei tribe silently gathered to present Dinah with a gift: a suit for battle, adorned with elements representing both Hu-Yuhar and Wonderland. As the women unfolded it before her, Dinah bit her lip to keep from bursting into tears of appreciation. Here she was taking these women's husbands and sons to fight for her— some surely to the death—and they were giving her a work of art, something that could never be repaid or replicated. The breastplate was a pure, flawless white that reflected the bright rays of the sun. Across the front was a red painted heart, slashed through with a single broken edge. It was very similar to her father's armor, only it had been bent and shaped to a woman's body. It came down and hit her at the hip, where tiny red hearts lined the sharp edging. They also gave her black leg and arm guards, marked with the same red heart.

The armor, while meticulously crafted, was just a fore-taste of their artistry and talent, shown fully in Dinah's cloak. To call it a cloak was a mistake, for it was so much more than that. It fastened around her neck and was buoyed out from her shoulders by the same remarkable light wood that held the Hu-Yuhar tents aloft. A thick collar of black-and-white checkerboard fabric fanned out from the sides of her neck and curled into two hearts just below her cheeks. The collar was lined with soft white gossamer feathers plucked from young birds and the cape was made of white crane feathers. The tip of each feather had been dipped in red paint, giving the appearance of a blood-tipped wing. The cape stretched out behind her like wings, long enough to brush the ground. Dinah let them dress her and braid her hair with ribbons. When they all stepped back, wide-eyed, she knew she was ready.

Dinah settled her ruby crown on her head and turned to face the women. Some were weeping, others looked simply afraid. As she emerged from her tent, Cheshire put his hand over his heart and gasped. Sir Gorrann, steps behind him, raised his eyebrows.

"How do I look?" asked Dinah with a smile.

Bah-kan was sharpening a knife on a small rock nearby and looked up in her direction. "Terrifying. A thing of nightmares."

"If *you* think that," she replied, "then they have done a fine job."

She gave a thankful nod to the Yurkei women, who gathered around and laid their hands over the heart on her breastplate, giving her healing tinctures and murmuring quiet prayers for her success.

That night, Dinah had barely returned to her tent before tears of gratitude fell heavily. There was little time for tears while the gears of war were turning, and she was grateful for their release.

The sun rose and set in the sky, and before Dinah felt she could wrap her head around all the details, it was the night before their departure. All of Hu-Yuhar fell silent, and Dinah could feel the heavy desperation and fear in the air—so much was at stake in this gamble that rested on *her*. The throne of Wonderland, the fate of a native people—it all weighed on her shoulders, heavy as the cape they had draped over her. As a dark night fell over Hu-Yuhar, so removed from those who clutched each other desperately in their tents, Dinah walked through the silent valley, making her way toward the stone cranes that guarded their whispered secrets. There was one more thing that she wanted.

Without the aid of her guards, Dinah climbed the ladder and entered Mundoo's tent. He was feasting with his family, and Dinah felt rude about interrupting this sacred last night at home. Still, she pushed open the flap and heaved to her feet as Mundoo's wife and seven children looked up in alarm.

"I need to speak with you before tomorrow."

Mundoo gestured with his hand, and his wife and children scampered out onto the bridges, which rocked loudly in the cool mountain air. Dinah lifted her fingers to the crown. Lately, whenever she felt the creeping doubts or the listless fear that had come with preparing for war and death, she touched her crown. It centered and reassured her. She gave a slight bow to Mundoo before she began speaking in a quiet yet forceful voice.

"You have something I want. I feel that we have given you a great deal in our negotiations. I have not asked for anything."

Mundoo laughed as he lustily licked the grease from his fingers. "You have asked for nothing. Nothing except a crown on your head and to become the most powerful person in Wonderland."

Dinah swallowed and continued. "I want him back. He is no good to you dead. We need him."

"No. *You* need him. A normal steed will fit you just fine."

"Any man who rides a Hornhoov knows that to be a lie."

Mundoo rose and sat stiffly on his throne of golden cranes. He looked at Dinah, amused. "I cannot give you the mad beast that has killed so many of my warriors. It goes against every principle of Yurkei justice that we have, even if I believe he would aid you in battle. The only reason we have kept him alive was to study him."

Dinah smiled. "I realize that, and I would never ask you to compromise your rule or reputation with your people. But what if I could offer you, and the Yurkei, something greater than death?"

Mundoo raised an eyebrow at her, his radiant blue eyes boosting what little confidence she had at that moment. "And what could that possibly be? What could possibly equal the cost of lives? Some of your Wonderland gold perhaps? A raid of your treasury once you are crowned?" he scoffed. "It is so like Wonderland to think they can buy Yurkei justice. You do not understand our way if you think gold can pay for blood."

Dinah opened her hands in a show of mercy. "Not money. I would give you life for death. It is the only thing that is greater."

Mundoo tapped his fingers above his lip. "My curiosity bids me to hear you out. Continue. But be careful that you don't insult me in my own tent, in my own kingdom. You are not my queen, Dinah—do not forget it." His eyes lingered on the hatch door that flapped open at the bottom of the tent. "It's a long flight down from the crane's wings."

Dinah bowed her head. "Once I am queen, I will breed Morte with your Hornhoov, Keres. You will get the first six of his foals, both male and female, which eventually you could breed as well."

Mundoo darted from his throne and grabbed Dinah's chin. "Do you take me for a fool, girl? Or are you the fool? With an army of Hornhooves, my tribe would quickly grow to be a threat to Wonderland Palace itself. How am I to believe that you will give me his offspring?"

"You have my word as queen."

"You aren't queen yet," he snapped. "How will I know that you will hold to your promise?"

Dinah felt the crown heavy upon her head. "I swear it on my brother's life, on Charles's name."

Mundoo released her. "Six Hornhoov foals for the Yurkei, brought to us when they are a year old to begin training."

Dinah nodded. "The first six. And not one more. The next six will be mine."

"And what if you do not become queen? That is quite likely you know."

Dinah was already climbing down the ladder. "Then we will all be dead anyway. Good night."

She found Morte in a pen as high as three men, lined with the strong white wood. This wood, however, was ringed with thorns, and she saw hundreds of tiny cuts along his legs and head. Morte had been so happy to see her that he only stomped around her three times as he threatened to crush her to death. Finally, once a puff of steam hissed from his nostrils, he let Dinah run a single finger down his massive nose. He lifted his knee so she could mount and jumped from the opened cage. They ran through the valley for hours, the thundering of his hooves scaring the other wild ponies into submission. Upon her return, the Yurkei presented her with a saddle built specially to ride a Hornhoov, originally built for the chief. It straddled Morte's neck, rather than his back, but it also had a groove where Dinah could sit on her knees if she so desired. With her beast, her saddle, and her crown, she led the army of a thousand Yurkei south, navigating a secret narrow path that wound down from the Yurkei Mountains, through the middle plain and into the Darklands. The path had led her here, to this pit of wet sorrow, astride Morte, proud and exhausted. Dinah looked now, out at the tents, silent in the morning air.

The black devil gave an impatient stamp of his hooves as she pondered what she came here for. What had Sir Gorrann said? *A conflict between two of the warriors, oh yes.* She climbed down from Morte, who gave an angry snort when she attempted to tie him to a pole. His saucer-sized eyes shimmered with anger. *Would she never learn?* Instead she dropped the reins and Morte galloped off. He would return when she needed him, dragging along a bloody carcass of some poor animal to place at her feet.

Dinah ducked into Sir Gorrann's tent. Cheshire, Sir Gorrann, and Bah-kan all stood silently as she peered curiously at each of them. Their faces were alarmingly happy.

"What are you staring at? Where are the warriors? Have they already killed each other?"

Cheshire let a devious smile creep over his face. "There are no warriors. Follow me." Without another word, he stepped out of the tent, with the two other men following.

"What?" Dinah ran to catch up with him, her sword bouncing across her hip. "Stop! I'm in no mood for a game right now! I think you have played enough with me for a lifetime."

Cheshire's grin stretched even wider, a naughty cat, caught in his deception. "I think you will much enjoy this game, Your Highness."

They were climbing a low grassy ridge, slick and wet from the evening mist. Dinah slipped a few times as she made her way up the rise, her boots squelching in dark water that ran uphill. "Have you found more rogue Cards? Send the ambassadors to speak with them at once."

"No," replied Cheshire. "Not *rogue* Cards." He stopped Dinah and held her by the shoulders. "Climb to the top of the crest and see what we have brought you, a gift to our queen from your loyal servants." He bent his head to her ear and whispered, "But mostly from me."

Sir Gorrann and Bah-kan hung back just before the crest of the hill. Dinah gave Sir Gorrann a strange look as she walked away from them. He gave a small nod, and so she continued climbing. The top of the hill looked out onto a low meadow, dotted with white mossy trees and small pools of still water. She squinted, unsure of what she was seeing. Her heart began hammering. Men. It was a line of hundreds of men, each armed, bearing the familiar uniform, black on black. A man on a large white horse led them forward. Dinah's breath caught in her throat. *Had she been tricked? Was this her father's doing? Had Cheshire played her?* The white horse was galloping toward her now, but it didn't move like a Hornhoov—he was too slow, and the rider was smaller, with a mane of curly brown hair blowing in the . . .

Dinah didn't feel her body start to move, but soon she was sprinting over the meadow, screaming his name, tears falling freely down her cheeks. She looked the opposite of a queen—a woman lost, a child coming home. There was no majesty, no decorum, only him, always him.

"WARDLEY! WARDLEY!"

He abandoned his horse, sprinting toward her as she screamed his name.

"WARDLEY!"

They collided in the middle of the field in a tangle of

limbs and a crushing embrace. Both fell to the ground, sobbing, pressed into each other with a breathtaking fierceness. Wardley was kissing her forehead, his arms wrapped tightly around her.

"I thought I would never see you again!" sobbed Dinah.

"I'm here now. I'm here. Shhh."

She raised her hands to his face, feeling his cheeks, his new beard. "It's you. You're safe." Dinah was babbling now, close to hysteria. "I'm sorry, Wardley, I'm sorry, please forgive me. Forgive me for hurting you, for stabbing you." She pressed her hand against where she knew his wound to be. "I'm so sorry!"

Wardley's eyed filled with tears. "You have nothing to be sorry for. I'm the one who is sorry. I'm a coward. I should have left with you. I should have found you sooner. You are the rightful queen. I should have protected you." Wardley crushed her close to his chest.

"You did, Wardley. You saved my life." They leaned their foreheads together, their hearts hammering loudly in the damp wind. Dinah wiped away her tears, suddenly aware of making a scene in front of throngs of armed men. "What are you doing here?" she whispered. Wardley looked down at her, his eyes the color of warm chocolate, eyes she had loved her entire life. Her heart was captivated by him, even after all this time.

"Dinah, don't you know? I'm here to command your army."

He grabbed her arm and pulled her to her feet. Dinah looked out at the sea of soldiers in black, all standing motionless: warriors, murderers, and prisoners. *The Spades had arrived.*

A smile crept across her face.

With these men, she could crush the king.

Twelve

Sleep was of paramount importance, yet Dinah couldn't think of anything she needed more than to feast her eyes on Wardley's slumbering face. She watched silently, mesmerized by the way his lips parted slightly with each deep breath.

After their joyous reunion and once they returned to camp, Dinah had seen how exhausted Wardley was. His lips were cracked and bleeding, and dark circles shadowed his eyes. He was thinner than Dinah had ever seen him, and there was a tortured ache present in his face that broke her heart. The Spades, eight hundred and seventy-two in number, had marched for a week under his leadership and arrived hungry, exhausted, and irritable. They possessed a begrudging respect for Wardley, but the Spades as a group were independent and unruly, and he held on to his command by the skin of his teeth and the ferocity of his blade. After he made sure that the men were settled into their makeshift tents, he promptly collapsed into Dinah's open cot and fell asleep within minutes. Dinah perched on a stool nearby, her hands folded together, her sword across her lap, her black eyes drinking in every breath of him. *He's here*, she thought. *He came for me. I wasn't wrong to believe he'd find me.* Wave after wave of relief washed over her, a flood of penetrating joy. It wasn't just that he was alive and unhurt—not on the surface, anyway—but that she had someone here she trusted without hesitation. Sir Gorrann was a fine companion, but Wardley had known Dinah her entire life, in the intimate way that only a childhood friend could.

She continued to watch him sleep until her own weariness closed her eyes. She awoke to Morte's impatient, thundering steps outside the tent. He was hungry; he was always hungry. Dinah found a live chicken and gave it to

Morte, who enjoyed chasing his prey around, toying with it, before he mercilessly speared it through the middle with one of the bone shards encircling his hooves. He then settled into the dirt to feast on its still-flailing body, and Dinah returned to the tent with a distaste for breakfast. Wardley, however, awoke starving, and Dinah couldn't feed him fast enough. She knelt by his bedside as he devoured dried bird meat, loaves of bread, and apples. Crumbs drifted down onto his long legs. His brown eyes bore into hers, overjoyed to see her, and yet filled with a terrible guilt. Wardley insisted that Dinah tell him everything, down to the last detail. She took a deep breath and recounted her story, alarmed at how dangerous everything seemed in retrospect. She started when she was awakened in her bed by a hand over her mouth and continued on through the details of Cheshire's affair with her mother. The night on the mountain with the cranes and the shadows she kept to herself. That moment was hers alone, concealed close to her heart, next to the place where she held Wardley. He watched her with amazement as she told her tale, his face reacting boldly to each turn. When she finished, he sat quietly for a few minutes before speaking.

"So Cheshire is your father?"

"So it would seem."

"And you believe him?"

"I don't have to believe him. I know it to be true. Look at him, and look at me. I looked nothing like my father—" Dinah corrected herself, something she was starting to do more often. "I'm sorry, the King of Hearts. I look nothing like the king. And I believe that my mother had an affair. When I was young I heard them arguing about it. There are so many things that fell together when he told me, so many disparate pieces that fit perfectly into place. My life makes sense now, even though the whole thing is a bit alarming."

Wardley was quick to see through her easy cadence. "A bit alarming?" he scoffed. "That's how you feel about Cheshire being your father?"

Dinah walked over to the tent flap and looked through the narrow sheaf of light. Thousands of tents littered the damp ground as far as she could see. "He's clever. He's organized this entire war, all to put me on the throne. He saved my life and probably will again. The king never even looked me in the eye. He hated me. He murdered Charles, Wardley."

His voice softened. "I know. Be wary that your gratitude doesn't turn into blind trust."

Dinah shook her head. "I won't. I promise." Cheshire was the least of her concerns. Right now there were a thousand Yurkei warriors, three hundred rogue Cards, and almost nine hundred Spades all gathered in one wet field. The Spades were the most loathed of all Cards among the Yurkei. If they all weren't careful, the war could start and end right here.

Wardley looked past her, casually resting a hand on her shoulder. "It's good to see you, Dinah."

Dinah's skin tingled at his touch, at being near to him. She forced herself to take a few quiet steps back into the tent.

"Sit down. You are exhausted and in no shape to be moving around. But tell me all that's happened in the palace since I've been gone."

"I'll tell you later. Right now I have to get ready to meet with the war council. Do you mind if I clean up?"

Dinah rolled her eyes. "I've seen you bathe a thousand times."

"That is true." Wardley crouched next to a small bowl

of water and pulled his shirt over his head. Dinah struggled to keep her face motionless as her eyes raked over his tan, taut skin and she watched with pleasure as he scrubbed the grime off his lean chest. As he lathered a bar of soap through his hair and scraped the dirt from under his fingernails, he repeated most of what she already knew: after she had stabbed him (way too deep! he was kind enough to remind her) he was transported to the infirmary, where the King of Hearts had found him and demanded his head. Wardley had assumed that he would die right there and then.

"He was mad with rage, Dinah, furious and insane. You've seen him drunk—well, this was a thousand times worse. He began striking the midwives and the nurses, screaming, 'Off with his head! Off with his head!'" Wardley shook his floppy hair. "I was terrified. I couldn't move. I couldn't fight. I could barely stay conscious, for gods' sake. Luckily, one brave doctor convinced him that my blood on the table was price enough. No man would let himself be injured that deeply on purpose. The king stuck his fingers deep into my wound to make sure."

"Oh, Wardley. I'm so sorry."

Wardley let the wet rag linger over the jagged, ugly scar on his shoulder, four inches long and barely healed. Dinah felt tears flood her eyes as she looked at the hideous wound she had inflicted. "I'll get you some Yurkei medicine for that. Their potions possess incredible healing powers." She let her fingers softly trace the scar before stepping away.

He paused. "Many times I woke up in the stables, not remembering that I had fallen asleep. The days seemed never ending, and the nights . . ." Wardley had a faraway look in his eyes, a look that Dinah had seen before—it was a place she could never reach him. His mind was elsewhere, and for a second she saw a flicker of *something* pass in front of them.

"Wardley." At the sound of her voice, he snapped back to attention, his eyes filled with tears.

"After a while Cheshire came to see me. He told me his plan, each week a bit more information—never enough that I could act on it alone, and never enough that I could ever accuse him of treason. He's crafty, Dinah."

So am I, she thought, *because he is my father*.

"Finally, the man told me what he wanted. He wanted me to lead an army of Spades south to meet you, here in the Darklands. To fight for the rightful queen, to fight for you." He smiled. "But I did not need convincing—you are the rightful Queen of Wonderland. I wondered: How do you convince an army of Spades to fight against their fellow Cards? What would make a single Spade drop their loyalty to one crown to fight for another?"

Dinah had no idea. Wardley leaned forward, a drop of water falling off a curly lock of brown hair. "*Rights*, Dinah. The Spades long for their own rights. As it turns out, I didn't have to convince anyone. They have been waiting for this for a long time. Our departure date was set, in the middle of a long night. I stole away from the stables and came to the place that Cheshire had told me, half-convinced that this was some sort of insane game that the king was play-ing to test my loyalty. But there they were in the darkness, a silent army of Spades just waiting in the courtyard, with their commander, Starey Belft, at the helm. Here's what I've learned, and what you should remember: the Spades' loy-alty is not to the king. It has never been to the king. It is to Starey Belft. He lives the depraved life of a Spade, and so they respect him. They would follow him into hell, and they did. We marched for a week and lost more than ten men. We only have a few horses. The things I've heard from these men, you wouldn't believe. . . ."

Sir Gorrann poked his head into the tent and looked surprised to see Wardley soaking wet and Dinah watching silently.

She smiled. "It's not what it looks like."

"I couldn't care less. The council is waiting for yeh both."

Dinah gave a slight nod. "We'll be there shortly. Thank you, Sir Gorrann."

He left, and Wardley eyed the door skeptically. "What about him? Do you trust him? You know he's in Cheshire's pocket, don't you?"

"Aside from you, I'm not sure there is anyone I fully trust, or ever will again. And yet I believe that Sir Gorrann has my best interests at heart. I consider him a dear, eternally grumpy friend."

Wardley pulled a ripped tunic over his head. He softly took Dinah's face in his hands and her heart stopped. "You do know what you are doing, don't you? You're planning a war, Dinah. A war in which many people will die, perhaps even yourself. This isn't playing swords in front of the stable. This isn't a game."

Dinah pulled back from him, her face flushed. Wardley always knew how to get under her skin. "Of course I know! I'm the rightful queen. Shouldn't I fight for my throne?"

Wardley shook his head. "You are, but I worry for you. You've never seen a battle, you've never seen a man . . ."

Dinah shoved him roughly backward, her anger surprising her. "What? I've never seen a man die? I've seen my brother's body crumpled on a stone slab. I've seen a farmer with an arrow buried in his back just because he happened to be near my path. I killed more than a few Cards on my way out of the palace, and I see their bloody faces in my dreams. So don't tell me that I haven't seen death or war, or that I don't know what I'm doing. I've been at war with the King of Hearts since the day that I was born."

Wardley grabbed her hands. "I'm sorry! You're right. I can't imagine what you've been through. Forgive me, my queen."

Dinah stared at him for a moment before nodding her

head. "Everyone thinks I am just a little girl, pretending she will be queen. But I will take my father's crown. I will." Her skin tingled with the idea.

Wardley sank to his knees. "You're right. I'm sorry for my presumptions. I have missed you, Dinah, deeply." He wrapped his arms around her legs, pressing his head against her knees. "Knowing your heart beats has given me new life and glorious purpose."

Dinah let her hand rest on his thick curls, her face cracking into a smile at his touch. Her hands slid down his hair, tracing his jawline, pulling his face upward so that his chin brushed the top of her thighs. "Wardley . . ."

Before she could go any further Wardley leaped to his feet.

"Dinah—you shoved me!" The boy she loved laughed a bit before stepping back and shaking his head, his eyes searching her furious face. "You are surely not the same girl that I kissed under the Julla Tree. You've grown strong!"

"Don't forget it," she snapped, resentful that Wardley had riled her heart up, as he always did.

She cleared her throat.

"Let's go, they are waiting for us."

Wardley gave her a look.

"Don't be mad. I'm sorry I doubted you." He reached out and tugged playfully on her braid, and Dinah's fierce heart melted.

Thirteen

The war council met in a circular black tent that sat squarely in the middle of all the other tents, a dark spot in a sea of clouds. Long onyx flags with the symbol of the Spades stitched haphazardly across their front panels snapped in the wind, blowing out from the tent pillars. Before the Spades had arrived, the war council's conversations had taken place over fires, or in regular tents. This tent was new, large, and intimidating. It carried a message: the Spades were not to be trifled with. As Dinah walked toward the tent with Wardley, several Spades bowed before her. Dinah felt a rush of pride as their heads tipped to the ground. *I will be their queen someday.*

Dinah ducked inside, Wardley behind her. A large table made of light wood filled up the room, forcing them to stand pressed against the soft black fabric of the tent. Rising up from the table stood a model of Wonderland Palace. Dinah marveled at its construction—every window, gate, and turret was present, each tiny shutter accounted for. She ran her fingers over the model of the stables, the rose garden, the Black Towers, and the iron walls that surrounded the city in a perfect circle. The hardened tips of her fingers rested on the Great Hall, and she looked up in amazement.

"How did you get this?"

"Allow me to answer that, Your Majesty." Starey Belft crept out of the corner, darkness hiding half of his scarred face. Dinah recognized him by his face, which she'd seen at various palace events, but also by his commander's brooch— it was black like all the Spades' insignias, but a single white diamond sparkled from the middle, denoting a higher rank. His face had been badly slashed during a battle with the Yurkei, but the other half remained ruggedly handsome. He looked tired and worn, with plum bruises underneath his eyes. Starey Belft was famous for his fierce loyalty to his troops and his love for loose women. He gave Dinah a wink with his good eye.

"You look well, Princess. You've lost your round baby cheeks."

"And you, sir."

"Eh, I look like I got slashed in the face with a knife."

There was a painful silence in the tent until Bah-kan burst out laughing. "Aye! You did!" Starey glowered at him.

Dinah motioned for him to sit. Each member of the council took a seat around the massive wooden castle. "Again, I will ask, how did you come across such a masterpiece?"

Starey Belft cleared his throat. "Ah, I took it, Your Majesty. When I knew we were leaving the palace and turning our loyalty to you, I broke into the king's chambers and took his model, piece by small piece." He demonstrated by breaking off half of the kitchens, folding it flat, and then putting it back into place.

"It's a puzzle!" exclaimed Dinah.

"It made it a bit easier to transport. Still, I don't think my Spades relished carrying it through the Darklands."

Dinah rested her hands on her lap. She didn't want to appear too eager. "How is it, Starey Belft, that you came to be in this tent today carrying the weight of the palace on your shoulders? It must be an incredible load to bear alone."

"It is, my lady." Starey took a long sip of the ale the Spades had brought with them. After all, who went to war without libations? She stared unflinchingly at him until he shrugged sheepishly. "What do you know about the life of a Spade, my lady?"

"I know that living the life of a Spade is an honor."

Starey jumped to his feet, his face flushed with anger and inches from hers. Everyone in the tent held their breath until he seemed to think better of his actions and turned away. When Dinah opened her mouth to speak, Starey Belft turned and spit, spraying the ale from his mouth all over Dinah. She coughed and wiped her eyes, willing the churning rage inside her to dissipate. Sir Gorrann stepped in front of her, his sword drawn and trembling as he pointed it at his old commander, a man Dinah knew he deeply respected.

"Yeh forget yerself, Commander! Sir, this is the future Queen of Wonderland, and yeh will respect her as such."

Starey Belft laughed. "Sit back down, Gorrann. I could skin you for treason, you know, you traitorous letch."

The men stared at each other as Dinah wiped the ale off her chest with her sleeve. Finally, Cheshire's voice boomed out from behind the wooden Black Towers, the height of the spires amplifying his disembodied voice over the tiny palace. "Both of you sit down. There will be no fighting in this tent, no skinning of anyone. Starey, if you are here, you must respect the queen. She understands that you've had a very long journey and that you weren't in your right mind when you happened to spill your ale near her feet."

"Spilled it out of his mouth," mumbled Wardley.

"It's fine," murmured Dinah, patting her hair with her sleeve. "I've had much worse."

Starey Belft's anger turned quickly to shame. "I'm sorry, Your Majesty. It's just that, if you think the Spades live a life of honor, you are mistaken. I should have expected that the daughter of the King of Hearts would never know the truth of our lives." Starey collapsed back into his chair. "In between birth and death, the life of a Spade is one of misery and sacrifice. We are considered the lowest ranking of the Cards, and are treated with disdain by the rest." He gave Wardley an accusatory glance. Spades had no love for Heart Cards. "As you know, Spades are not allowed to marry or have children. When we take our oaths, we are sworn to live for Wonderland Palace, so why would we have a need for women, love, or comfort? Spades live in the freezing barracks that lie just behind the Black Towers, stacked one on top of the other, so that you never know whose piss you'll be standing in when you wake up. We have a place to sleep and food to eat, but nothing more. When Hearts, Clubs, or Diamonds go home, what do they return to? A room in the palace? A wife, a son? We return to nothing but the cold and the darkness." Starey gave a shiver.

"I don't care what the official stance of the palace is, but there is something that permeates the ground near the Black Towers. The black roots run through our sleeping quarters. It makes men angry. And just when we seem to have unity, the prisoners come. Straight from the Black Towers, released to the Spades to serve the realm. Murderers, thieves, liars, rapists—that's who the king sends to make up his army. How are we ever to rise above our rank when our barracks are constantly being filled with the dregs of society? We cannot, which is just how the king likes it."

He exhaled and sat back on his wooden stool, taking a long sip of the swirling golden ale. "The life of the Spade, my lady, is *not* 'honorable' as you say. No, it's filled with fighting and bickering among ourselves, for we have nothing to do but the King of Heart's dirty work. It is a miserable existence. We are asked to live in this constantly changing darkness, and yet, if the king needs someone assassinated, who does he come to?" Starey beat his breast with a gloved fist. "He comes to me to murder his enemies, to seek out Yurkei spies, to dispose of his mistresses when he grows tired of them. I have thrown men in prison who simply looked at the man in a way he did not like. I do these things, and for what? To see my men treated like sewage, discarded like day-old tarts?"

He brought his fist down onto the wooden palace and the stables crumpled beneath his hand. "Tell me, Your Majesty, what will my legacy be? A legacy of death and sorrow, praying that war will come, just so we may take leave of our sorry quarters? I tell you, no! If it is the last thing I do in this pathetic world, I will leave the Spades in a better position than they are in now. My men deserve better than this excuse for an existence, for we are the ones who fight and die for this kingdom."

Bah-kan spoke up from the corner of the tent where he softly ran a dagger across his giant cheek. "You fight and die for unjust wars. The Yurkei have done nothing to deserve your raids. Your men are brutish and cruel—they are monsters."

"I will not listen to a coward speak," replied Starey Belft, his face stoic.

Bah-kan leaped up with a roar, and Dinah barely had enough time to fling herself between the two men.

"STOP! As your queen, I order you to step back!"

The men, their chests heaving, took a single step back, more out of self-preservation than respect, Dinah suspected.

Bah-kan eyed Dinah as he spoke. "You are not my queen; the Yurkei have never submitted to Wonderland domination. But I am sworn to protect you, as Mundoo commanded. Do not forget, little girl, that is why I obey you now."

Dinah nodded and waited until Starey and Bah-kan sat

back down, her patience gone. "Sir Starey, what demands have you brought on behalf of the Spades? What price will I pay to have them fight for me?"

Starey handed Wardley a rolled piece of paper, which Wardley then gave to Dinah. "It's all written there for you, made up of the voices of a thousand Spade warriors that have been oppressed and enslaved for centuries. We have five demands. First, a Spade shall be allowed to marry and raise children. Second, a Spade can choose to live with his family in a private household within the kingdom, as do all the other Cards." He paused. Dinah nodded. These seemed reasonable. "Third, we would ask that you move our barracks away from the Black Towers, to the south side of the kingdom, as the first major project once you are crowned queen. Fourth, we ask that the queen would meet with a small group of established Spades before declaring war or ordering raids on any group of people. We would like to have a say in the matter before we are asked to sharpen our axes for battle. Our final demand is that the Spades will take new rank just under the Heart Cards, and be paid accordingly. This will allow us to afford more for training and feeding, so that we may build a strong army, inside and out."

Dinah faced him across the wooden structure. "If this war works, Sir Starey, there will be no need for raids or battles. We seek peace with the Yurkei."

"A strong queen needs a strong army."

"He is right, Your Majesty," spoke Cheshire. "Though you will not war any longer with the Yurkei, you will still need an army to police the city and to protect you. Especially once you have established your rule, there will be parties who seek to harm you." *Like the Diamonds and the Clubs*, thought Dinah, *who will have just been usurped by the Spades. I will elevate one group to make two others angry.*

Perhaps this was the game that Wardley had spoken of. War was, at its most basic level, the great reassigning of positions—a king who could become a prisoner, a princess who could become a casualty of war. It occurred to Dinah that her war might not be over once the king was dead. There would be many sacrifices made in order to win, and many of them would make the pillars of Wonderland society very unhappy. Dinah tucked the scroll into her tunic.

"I will think on your demands, Sir Starey. For now I

would encourage you to take a needed rest and sober up. We have much planning to do. We will meet back here this evening, just after dinner is served."

The war council rose to its feet and bowed before Dinah exited the tent. Cheshire trailed behind her. Dinah handed the scroll to him. "Please look over these and make sure there are no tricky loopholes. Return it to me so that I may look over it again by tonight."

Cheshire rested his hand on her shoulder. "You did well in there, my queen. I am so proud of you, as both your humble servant and your father."

Dinah felt unsure of how to respond and so she strode away from him, toward Morte, who stood waiting for her beside her long white tent, which someone had haphazardly painted with a red slashed heart. "I'm going for a short ride to clear my head. Please have it read when I return."

Cheshire bowed, a feline smile stretching across his thin face. "Nothing would please me more, Your Majesty."

"Sir Gorrann!"

"Yes?"

"Please join me for a short ride."

Cheshire's smile disappeared. Sir Gorrann gave her a half salute with his hand. "With pleasure. I need to fetch Cyndy."

Morte began to nip at the tent as he pawed the ground impatiently. His hooves brought ripples up from the grassy surface, where the water underneath sloshed and bubbled. "I'll meet you at the blighted ponds. He cannot wait."

Dinah bowed her head with reverence once she reached Morte, and he lifted his leg for her to vault onto his back. Morte ran with abandon for the blighted ponds. Dinah relished the damp wind on her face as they flew across the wet valley. The ponds were not far, which was convenient, for it was where the army drew their water. Alongside the clear, delicious pools of perfectly cool water, there were other ponds, the blighted ponds. She had seen them almost every day in the Darklands and even now stared at them with amazement. The murky pinkish waters were topped with a foamy froth that looked delicious, but smelled atrocious. Every now and then a creamy, shimmering bubble would rise up from the fathoms below. Bordering on the edge of the moss, the bubble would creep a few feet over the ground and then float slowly toward the nearest living creature. They were easy to avoid if one watched out for them, for they drifted at a snail's pace; but if they touched the skin, as one unfortunate Yurkei warrior had found out, they burst open, bathing the unfortunate victim in a warm splash of effervescent pink. Seconds later, skin, blood, and veins would begin to turn white and harden. The warrior was left petrified within minutes, a creamy pink bubble formed over his lips. The Yurkei had been afraid to touch him to give him a proper burial, and so they had left his body behind in the ponds. The next day when they had returned to gather water, the warrior's body was gone, and in its place was a new rosy pocket of water. It had consumed him, and he had become whatever had eaten him from the inside.

Dinah watched with caution as Morte drank mightily from one of the clear pools. There were no roaming bubbles so far, but she could see the blighted ponds rippling in the distance, a sea of foamy pink bubbles against the green moss.

"I hate this place." Sir Gorrann rode up beside her, his mare panting with exhaustion. He looked over at Morte as Dinah dismounted him. "Gods, he's fast. Cyndy here was galloping her fastest, and we were still at least a half mile behind you."

Dinah smiled and rested her hand on Morte's chest. He shot her an annoyed look and stepped away. "He wasn't even truly running. When the king chased us, he was running so fast I could barely make out the landscape."

"Mmm. He's an incredible monster, isn't he?" They both glanced over at Morte as he happily stomped a toad to death.

Dinah trained her eyes on the ever-shifting ponds. "Tell me, Sir Gorrann, what do you think of the Spades' demands? This is why you agreed to find me, right? Why you said you would work with Cheshire? *This* was your agenda. You wanted to make sure that I survived and made it to the right people so that I could advance the cause of the Spades. Is that correct?"

He looked out into the distance. "Yeh would be correct. I never hid that I had an agenda, not from yeh. If I can't bring back Ioney and my Amabel, at least I can better the lives of those men who I would call brothers. But I will fight for yeh, Dinah. I believe that yeh will be a great queen, and

I will fight even if yeh don't agree to the Spades' demands. They are fair demands. There was nothing that seemed . . . in excess." He paused and took a sip of water from one of the clear ponds. "Of course," he continued as he wiped his mouth, "if yeh don't accept the Spades' demands, yeh will not have an army. On our side of the battle, we will have a thousand Yurkei warriors, three hundred Rogue Cards—— who are useless if yeh ask me—and the king will wipe all of yeh from Wonderland like the dirt under his feet."

"Can we win with the Spades?" Dinah asked.

Sir Gorrann watched with a wary eye as two champagne bubbles began drifting toward them, so light and friendly on the wind. "Perhaps. Mundoo was counting on them joining us when he marched north."

Dinah narrowed her eyes. "I wish I would have known."

"'Twas a gamble in the first place, even for Cheshire. Yeh should just be thankful that they are here now. Without them, we haven't a prayer. The Cards don't fear the Yurkei near as much as they should, but they will fear a line of Spades."

"Then it is done." Dinah watched a pretty pink bubble

burst across a low rock. Within seconds, the moss covering its surface shriveled and turned white. "And when you are allowed to marry, will you marry again, Sir Gorrann?"

He looked out at the low valley, now filled with several dozen floating pink bubbles, all very slowly making their way toward them. "For many of us, there is only one person who can fill the space of our heart."

Dinah thought of Wardley, the way his breath had washed across her face, the way the scar on his shoulder had stretched when he raised his arms to wash his body. She loved every part of him. For her, there was no other. "Yes."

His gold eyes rested on her face, the crinkles around them showing the first signs of a smile. She snapped her fingers for Morte, who didn't come, so she began walking quickly toward him.

"Thank you for your input, Sir Gorrann. I think we should head back to camp."

He watched a shimmering bubble that rolled slowly toward his feet. "Couldn't agree more."

Dinah looked out over the landscape, so enchanting, a

world of soft pink bubbles and warm light. She shrugged. "It feels like love."

"And that's why it'll kill yeh," replied Sir Gorrann, nudging her toward Morte.

Fourteen

Dinah's army continued to march toward Wonderland Palace and preparations for war continued at a frantic pace. When they weren't traveling, Dinah was meeting with the council, poring over Wonderland's laws or training with Bah-kan and Sir Gorrann. Wardley now brought his own special expertise into the bouts, and when they had fought tonight, Dinah was left spent and flushed.

Most nights the future queen fell into bed exhausted to the core. Her body ached, her mind was spent, and she wished she had insisted on bringing the heavenly grass mattress from Hu-Yuhar instead of this makeshift cot. Usually, a deep sleep took her immediately, but not this night. Her thoughts were lingering on Wardley, the way he had turned when she had lunged at him, the way his white sleeves fluttered when he spun, the droplet of sweat on his brow. The more aggravated she became the less likely sleep was, and she found herself tossing needlessly on her cot. *Something* was keeping her awake. There was a voice trailing on the edge of the warm wind. *Come to me.* Dinah tossed and turned. Sleep was a white rabbit on quick feet, and no matter how much she tried, she could not follow it into the blissful dark.

Exasperated, Dinah sat up and pulled on her tunic and boots. The damp air of the Darklands was growing warmer each day as summer neared and she had no need for heavy wool or feathered pants. She grabbed a handful of apple rinds from an open bag and ducked out of her white tent. Her two guards were, of course, wide-awake when she passed them outside.

"Your Majesty?" Ki-ershan was the only Yurkei warrior who addressed her as his queen. Dinah had grown quite fond of him.

"I'm just going for a short walk through the tents."

"You may not go alone."

"I won't. I'll have Morte with me."

The guard glanced up at the massive beast that had trotted over to greedily consume the sugar cubes. The bone spikes that protruded from his hooves were as white as the moon in the flickering torchlight.

"Are you sure, my lady?"

Dinah touched his shoulder. "It's just a walk, I promise. I'll be back in half an hour. I'll just be inside the Yurkei camp."

Normally the guards would not let her out of their sight unless she had a protector—Sir Gorrann or Wardley or Cheshire would serve well enough—but what could these men do that Morte could not? Dinah began strolling up and down the rows, first through the black Spade tents, which reeked strongly of men, ripe sweat, and ale. Loud snores filled the narrow grassy corridors, and Dinah smiled at each resonating snort. She lightly touched the tent flaps as she walked by, lingering on how close she felt to these soldiers. These men would fight and die for her, even if they weren't sure about her ability as queen. They believed in her, in her claim for the throne, but most important they believed she would acknowledge their rights. Whatever the reason, she would appreciate every sleepy sound that came from their filthy mouths. After the battle, there would be far fewer voices to hear.

A large field separated the Yurkei tents from the Spades. Morte galloped across it with abandon and waited impatiently for her on the other side. The Yurkei tents were vastly different from the Spade tents. The Yurkei tents were circular and white, utterly without color or flags. They hovered above the ground, buoyed up by thin wooden reeds.

The night was still and damp, the stars clustered in one small corner of the sky. Just out of the corner of her vision, Dinah caught the slightest flickering of purple light. She blinked. It was still there, a flash in the dark, a glow where there shouldn't be, pulsating from between two tents. Taking a few steps back, Dinah walked close to the line of white structures and peered between two that were situated abnormally close together. Between the two tents sat another, only this tent was almost a perfect circle—a sphere with a wide bottom, balancing precariously on two long wooden poles. Hazy lapis light pushed out from the tent. A trail of bluish lavender smoke exited through a hole in the top of the tent, winding and curling in on itself. Morte gave a loud snort and began bucking unhappily. The ground shook when his massive hooves met it, and she feared he would wake the entire army. Dinah reached for him.

"Shhh . . . shhhh . . . it's okay." Morte yanked back from her touch and galloped a few feet before he knelt to the ground. He stared at her accusingly. Dinah turned back to the tent, her curiosity piqued. This was the tent of Iu-Hora, the Caterpillar, the alchemist who created the incredible medicines that healed the Yurkei so quickly. He had potions and herbs for every ailment, several of which Dinah had used in her time at Hu-Yuhar. He was said to be many things—mad, a genius, an evil incarnation of the Yurkei's power and myth. Some said he hatched from a cocoon, others that he was brought down to the tribe by cranes. Each Yurkei either loved or feared him, dependent upon whether or not his medicines had been used to save their lives. Either way, he was guarded fiercely from the rest of Wonderland by the Yurkei. It was said that he held the secrets to the world within the confines of his pipe.

Recently, Dinah had heard whispers that Mundoo had sent Iu-Hora south with Dinah so that his potions might be used to sway the opinions of the Spades if needed. It hadn't been, but the idea that one could drug an army into doing one's bidding was disturbing. Dinah blinked in the hypnotic light, unsure of how long she had been staring at the tent. It reminded her of a glistening, opulent blueberry, and she found herself drifting toward it, not unlike her reaction in the mushroom field. *Stop it!* she told herself. *Be wise!* She spun on her heels to leave when a soft voice beckoned from the darkness, sweet like honey and heavy like wool.

"Come to me, Dinah, my child! Let me know who you are."

Morte gave a snort of unhappiness from across the field. The tent pulsed again with the light and Dinah found herself taking the steps up the wooden platform and entering. It took a few seconds for her eyes to adjust to the strange light, which she realized was coming from a large hookah pipe in the middle of the tent. It was almost as tall as Dinah herself. The glass of the hookah was transparent and, inside, silver-and-blue-veined leaves flickered and glowed. A thick smoke filled her eyes and lungs, and she instantly began to cough and choke.

"Take a deep breath, little queen. Let it fill you. Only then will you be able to see and hear your future. Or answer the question *who are you?*"

Her eyes cloudy, Dinah was barely able to see the outline of the massively fat Yurkei man who sat perched on a pile of bright pillows. His girth hung over the sides of the cushions, and only a yellow feather loincloth stood between her and his complete nakedness. His skin was dark and shiny and, unlike most Yurkei, completely unmarked by white lines. On the side of the tent, hundreds of clay pots and hanging scales all clamored for space. Iu-Hora noticed her staring with interest at his work.

"The Darklands have provided a most bountiful crop on which to experiment. I have already made three new potions since we've been here! One for rashes, one for aging eyes, and one for . . . well, you don't need to know that. You'll see."

She looked over at him again, but was unable to make

out his face. It kept shifting and changing, but that was just the hazy light, wasn't it? *Wasn't it?* She was very confused. Dinah felt the smoke make its way into her lungs, and a pleasant warm sensation began to stir under her rib cage. She was feeling very light, very free, very happy.

"Here. Take a smoke." Out of nowhere, a chubby hand extended the end of the hookah pipe to her. "Just one taste, Princess. Just one taste and hear what Iu-Hora has to tell you."

Dinah took the pipe and inhaled deeply, before she could think about the decision. Then she heard Sir Gorran's words echoing in her head. "Impulsive, just like your father." But that man wasn't her father. Or was he? She couldn't remember, and didn't seem to care. The smoke went down sweet and tingly, and she immediately felt like she was bursting with joy. Her head was clear, and her ears were open. She collapsed with a giggle onto a pile of pillows nearby.

"Did you get these from Wonderland? The Yurkei don't have pillows like this."

"They came to me how they came to me. You did not come here to ask questions about the pillows. You came here to ask much more difficult questions. And I am here to ask you . . . who are you?"

"I'm Dinah," she answered. "And I do not know why I'm here."

"You are here because I brought you here. I have been waiting a long time to meet the Queen of Hearts."

"I'm not queen yet."

He seemed to slither around her. "Ah, yes, war. The great coming war. A war that will change the fate of Wonderland. Blood, smoke, and birds. A deck of cards, falling . . . falling. I see a loaf of bread, a bloody sword, a fractured heart."

His words made no sense to Dinah. She laughed and then felt suddenly somber. "Can you see the outcome? I hear the Caterpillar is a predictor of fortunes."

For no clear reason, Dinah started laughing at the word *fortunes*. It was so amusing, that word.

"I cannot see the outcome of the war, because it involves the fate of too many. My visions are blurry with so many souls to see. I see much death and unhappiness. I see a beautiful woman weeping at a window, a skilled arrow, blue stars in the sky. I see you riding a black devil, with great wings stretched behind you."

"That would be Morte." Dinah laughed until she wept. She looked around. How long had she been laughing? A minute? Three hours? The Caterpillar emerged from the hazy light, his features still unreadable aside from his glowing blue eyes. It was all she could see. Dinah was suddenly terrified.

What are you doing? Get back. Don't touch me! She thought the words, but for some reason could not make her mouth form the sounds. Slowly, his fingers reached inside her tunic, and then he spun her around. For a moment Dinah was afraid of what was happening, but then she felt the pressing of his fingers against the scar on her shoulder.

"This was my work. A scar left on a queen by a chief. Something that she will never forget, but a sting that healed quickly." A substance was seeping through her skin from his fingers. She could feel it alternating hot and cold, tingling against her shoulder. It was inside of her, whatever it was, passing through her skin like water. Iu-Hora spun her back around and suddenly Dinah felt like she was floating with him, up through the tent into the stars that looked down on dead Charles. They were flying through the sky now, over the Darklands, over the fields. They flew up, up, and away until they hovered above Wonderland Palace. The Black Towers shimmered with wickedness below. She blinked. No. She wasn't in the sky. *Was she?* She was in the tent, and his blurry face was inches from her own, his hands on her face. Iu-Hora's voice changed as he leaned forward as if to kiss her, and she felt the thick smoke from his mouth wash over her face. All the smoke was suddenly sucked out of the circular tent and there was nothing but darkness, nothing but the heat of his forehead against hers and the sharp blue of his eyes. A low, terrible voice boomed out from the blackness. It belonged to Iu-Hora, but it didn't sound like him. Dinah found herself more afraid than she had ever been.

"*Queen of Hearts, the daughter of two fathers, heed my words. You will pierce the heart of one man and cut out the heart of the one you love most. Follow the crumbs to find your throne and only then shall your head rest in the grass.*"

Iu-Hora gave a silent intake of breath and suddenly blue smoke trailed out of his lips. His voice returned to normal and a silly giggle filled the tent.

"Would you like more, my queen?" Dinah pushed him backward into the pots and scales, which went crashing down under his massive weight. She wasn't sure what was happening. Blue smoke was pouring out of her mouth, changing colors as she breathed. Red morphed into a fiery orange, which curled into a pale blue, then a misty gray. Coughing, she crawled toward the tent flap.

"Come back!" he cried, laughing. "I have so much more to show you!"

She was running now, away from the tent, smoke pouring from her eyes, ears, and throat. It steamed out of her skin. She stumbled and fell to the ground. His voice returned and whispered in her ear, although she was nowhere near him.

"Keep your temper, Queen of Hearts."

Morte was beside her now, and she weakly pulled herself upward, stepping on his hoof, one of his bone shards giving her a thin cut on her ankle. She flopped over his back, lying facedown across him as she continued to choke on the colored smoke pouring from her mouth and nose. Morte began running back to her tent. Dinah's body was shuddering as if it had forgotten how to function. She was alternately freezing and stifling hot, and her mind was racing, making illogical jumps. Was she up or down? Where was she? After what seemed like years, Morte arrived in the Spades' camp and came to a violent stop in front of her tent. Yur-Jee and Ki-ershan leaped to their feet and gathered a shaking Dinah from his back. They babbled frantically in Yurkei, their voices so loud to Dinah's ears.

"Iu-Hora! No Wonderlander has ever been in his presence! What did he give her? Witch doctor! Pure evil!"

Wild hallucinations ran through Dinah's mind, and she heard pieces of Iu-Hora's words again: *"Daughter of two fathers . . . pierce the heart of one man . . . cut out the heart of the one you love most . . . follow the crumbs to find your throne. . . ."*

As the guards spoke in rapid Yurkei, Dinah heard Wardley's voice ringing above the commotion. "What the hell happened? Give her to me! Bring Cheshire now!"

Wardley cradled her against his chest, and she was aware that he was carrying her inside her tent. A thin trail of maroon smoke curled out of her lips, and Dinah blew it lovingly at his face. She struggled to stay awake. Wardley leaned his face over hers. "You can close your eyes, Dinah. I'm here." With a sigh, she surrendered, happy to fall asleep in the arms of the one she loved most.

Fifteen

Dinah slept the entirety of the next day, accompanied by the most vivid and bizarre dreams she had ever had. She would wake drenched in a sweat that pushed itself out of her skin in a swirl of vibrant colors, to find Cheshire and Wardley staring down at her, discussing things that she could barely understand.

"When will she be fully aware?"

"Hopefully the tea will draw out the hallucinatory effects of the smoke."

"Did they find him?"

"The Yurkei are guarding him day and night. We will not do anything. Actually, I think he might be of great use to us."

"Has Mundoo been notified of what his witch doctor did to the queen?"

"We sent two riders this morning with the message. They also carried our finalized plans for the battle. God help us if they are caught."

"They won't be. They're Yurkei."

Dinah would listen for what could have been hours or seconds before drifting back into her dazzling sleep. The next day, she woke to a cool cloth being pressed against her forehead.

"Your Majesty?" She looked up, hoping to see Wardley, but instead found herself uncomfortably close to Cheshire's face. "How are you feeling?"

Alarmed, Dinah pushed herself up faster than she should have and was rewarded with a bout of nausea. "Oh. Oh." She allowed herself to sink back into the cot. "What happened?"

Cheshire resumed lightly patting her head with the

cloth. "What do you remember?"

"I was out walking because I couldn't sleep . . . and I found Iu-Hora's tent." She frowned. "And then . . . then . . ." She should have remembered, but there was a gaping hole in her memory; it was puzzling and unnerving. She could see bits and pieces, but the knowledge of what had happened was missing. "I'm sorry . . . ," she sputtered. "I don't really remember. There was smoke and light and . . ."

Cheshire made a disgusted sound, yet his face showed a certain delight and fascination. "The Yurkei witch doctor has more powers than Wonderland has ever bothered to fathom. I highly doubt that you wandered there *entirely* on your own accord. He's been known to call those to him when he feels the need, whether by injury or trance. There is evil in that tent that might be of use to us yet. He has a mastery of alchemy that Wonderland has yet to discover." He stroked Dinah's hair softly, attempting to soothe her. It made her uncomfortable. "We almost lost you to the fever. If you had died, Iu-Hora's head would have been sucked down into the shadow ponds by now. You have caused a great stir, daughter."

Heads . . . *something about her head* . . . Dinah couldn't remember. There was only the unclear memory of smoke and light, and a burning deep in her lungs.

"Do you feel well enough to sit up now?"

"Yes." Dinah hated depending on him for anything, but she let him help her up and hold her hand as she gently made her way to a small wooden table. Soup steamed in a small mug and, somehow, there was a pile of warm sweets waiting for her. She looked up at Cheshire with amazement. "How does one make *warm pies* in the wilderness?"

He shrugged nonchalantly. "There is nothing I can't get for you." Cheshire raised a spoon to her lips.

"I can do it myself, thank you." Dinah clutched the spoon with determination and shakily brought it to her dry lips. "How did you get the—was it poison?—out?"

Cheshire leaned back on his chair and folded his long hands under his chin. "Wild Lavender rice tea. Rice attracts moisture, and the smoke, when inhaled, became a form of liquid hallucination. It's quite fascinating. I visited the witch doctor myself after I saw you, and he explained its full effects. My dagger at his throat helped a bit, I think. After that, the Yurkei wouldn't let anyone come near his tent." He paused. "I hate to be the one to tell you, but this incident only served to fan the flames of anger between the Spades and the Yurkei."

"We're on the same side for gods' sake," snapped Dinah. "Either way, many of these men will die for me. You would think that would be enough to bond them."

His smile faded. "That's where you are mistaken. These men do not fight and die for you. No man fights or dies for a leader. He dies for an ideal. The Spades will die fighting for their rights, for the right to have children, for a chance to live forever through their heirs. The Yurkei fight to reclaim the land of their forefathers." Distracted by a sweet on the table, he summed it up, "Don't delude yourself, these men fight wholly for themselves."

Cheshire selected a slice of plum pie and took a small bite. Dinah had never noticed how small and sharp his teeth were. His bites were half the size of hers. "Part of becoming a leader is learning how to manipulate that belief. It's the way power works. Your face and dress and crown represent these things for them, but it wouldn't matter if it was you or another. Your task now is to become a queen they'd be willing to die for."

Dinah stared at the ground. She had behaved so foolishly by going to Iu-Hora's tent, and yet, she was furious at him for pointing out the truth. "Ironic how you can speak of sacrifice with such ease when you only looked after your own interests while the king beat my mother and treated me with contempt."

Cheshire flashed a pitying grin at her. "Poor girl. Is that what you believe? I simply see it as keeping your best interest at heart. I would have loved nothing more than to steal you and your mother away in the dead of night and start over, away from the king, where I could love you both proudly. And yet, by doing that, I would deny you the crown, a chance to become the most esteemed person in Wonderland. Instead, I suffered in silence, watching the love of my life be touched by a man who disgusted me, and watching my daughter be raised by a man who hated her."

Cheshire slowly folded his napkin, taking care with each corner. When he was done, a tiny paper mouse remained. He set it inside her empty teacup before standing to leave. He calmly tucked in his purple tunic, then suddenly leaned over her menacingly. His sweet breath swept over her face. "Do not presume to know me, Dinah. I have sacrificed *everything* to get you where you are. And instead of being grateful for my sacrifice, and the sacrifice of all the men here, you repay us by wandering right into the arms of a mad witch doctor so that we might have watched you die slowly. You are not a child anymore. You are a queen, so behave like one!"

He stood up and took a deep breath, adjusting his brooch as he transformed himself back into the smooth, unruffled Cheshire. "Make sure that you don't do anything strenuous today. No sparring. No fighting. Wardley or Sir Gorrann is to be with you at all times. I don't trust your Yurkei guards anymore."

Dinah watched in simmering silence as Cheshire whisked himself out of the tent. Her appetite had disappeared. *He was right.* It was time to quit playing these risky games to satisfy her childish curiosity. She was no longer a girl sneaking into the Black Towers with Wardley. Her kingdom was at war, and she was too indulgent of her own whims. The consequences of her actions would be real and severe. For gods' sake, she had almost started a war here in their camp.

I will remember that, she thought. *I will remember that what the queen does matters. I will listen to Cheshire's wisdom, no matter how strange he makes me feel.* Deep in thought, she munched quietly on a blueberry tart. As she went to take another bite, she looked down in shock at the tips of her fingernails. They were a deep orange, stained with the poison that was slowly seeping out of her body, a real reminder of how close she had come to ruining the lives of thousands. She didn't believe that Iu-Hora, the witch doctor, had intended to kill her, and yet, he was dangerous just the same. Alone in the tent, Dinah closed her eyes and vowed that she would no longer make impulsive decisions on whatever whim came over her at the time. The cause and the crown came first. *I will become the queen they deserve.*

She guzzled cool water from a nearby bucket and lay down for a few more hours before she felt ready to stand and walk. When she finally left the tent, bright sunlight blazed down on her through the mist of the Darklands. Wardley was waiting for her, his long legs folded beneath him as he balanced his sword on one finger. "You're up!" His long arms wrapped around her shoulders, and Dinah gladly let him pull her against his body. "Come here, you idiot! I was so worried. Why did you go to Iu-Hora? Haven't you heard the rumors about him? They say he grinds up the bones of his people to fertilize their mushroom fields. What were you thinking?"

"I don't know. It was foolish, and it won't happen again," replied Dinah calmly. "And no, I hadn't heard that." She pressed her face against his shoulder. "Though I do not doubt it."

"What happened in there? What did you see?"

"I can't remember."

Wardley made a doubtful face.

Dinah sighed. "It's hard to explain—it's like someone has pulled a black cloth over that memory. I know he told me something important, but I cannot remember what it was, only traces of words." *Throne. Crumbs. Grass.* "It's there, I just can't reach it."

Wardley stepped back and took stock of her body. "How

well do you feel? Are you sure you shouldn't be lying down?"

Dinah shook her head. "No. I've been sleeping most of the day. I don't deserve any more rest, especially when my men are so busy." All around the camp was a flurry of activity. Horses were being fitted for breastplates. Swords were being sharpened, and the sound of metal on metal was deafening. During the day the camp was usually filled with the raised voices of men, but today there were no voices to be heard, only the sound of work and progress. All these sounds fell under an eerie quiet that permeated the air.

"Why is no one speaking?" Dinah saw several Spades cast fascinated looks in her direction and then drop their eyes when she looked back. "What's going on?"

Wardley looked at her quizzically before pushing her hair aside to whisper in her ear. Dinah's heart beat rapidly as his breath brushed her cheek. "Tomorrow we begin our march north, Dinah. The war is upon us."

The time she had missed in the Caterpillar's fog had left her confused. He was right—they would march out the following day, headed for Wonderland Palace. How had it arrived so suddenly? The Spades continued to stare at her.

"Move along!" Wardley snapped, and they begrudgingly obeyed.

"Why were they staring at me like that?"

"Probably because you are the only woman in this camp." He fidgeted awkwardly.

"Tell me the truth," ordered Dinah. She had known Wardley long enough that it was painfully obvious when he was lying.

He sighed. "Cheshire has been telling everyone how you survived the encounter with the Yurkei witch doctor, how in return he gave you a vision of our victory."

Dinah looked at Wardley and gasped. *"That is a lie!"*

He clamped his hand over her mouth. "Shh. It doesn't matter. It gives the men hope, letting them believe that you have some special knowledge of a victorious battle. Who knows, it might even be true. The men will have less fear when they go into battle if they believe fate is on their side."

Dinah grabbed Wardley's arm. "That is a false hope. There was no word of our victory. Although . . ."

Throne. Crumbs. Grass.

"There might have been," Dinah admitted. "I can't remember. Still, I want the men to believe in themselves, not some false prophecy. They need to have faith that we can win."

"And why exactly will we win?" asked Wardley.

"Because we are on the right side," answered Dinah, unconvinced. "Because we have to."

Dinah looked out over the camp. She knew the odds. Her men were outnumbered and perhaps outmatched. The Yurkei and the Spades would fight with a certain fervor, but did fervor and righteousness matter when the numbers were not in their favor? Dinah felt a fresh stab of fear. "Do you believe we can win? As the onetime future Knave of Hearts, do you think we will win?"

Wardley glanced down at Dinah, his face painted with weariness as a lock of curly brown hair fell over his eyes. Dinah felt her heartbeat quicken. "Take a walk with me, Dinah. There's something I want to show you."

Sixteen

Morte dutifully followed Corning, Wardley's obedient white steed, out of the camp and into the wilds of the Dark-lands. They walked in silence for about an hour, through hot swamps and over a field of strange rubbery plants that produced in Dinah an uneasy feeling of being watched. The plants unfurled themselves toward Morte's hooves as they passed by them before recoiling, rejected and hungry. As the valleys grew wetter and wetter, Wardley turned them slightly east, and the horses began a laborious climb up slick grassy hills, their hooves slipping on the slimy moisture that permeated the ground. Before long, the rolling peaks ended at a tangled bramble patch that defended itself from invaders with wicked-looking black thorns, each the size of a hand. They dismounted their steeds. Wardley tied Corning to the bush and Dinah simply dropped Morte's reins. He slashed at the bramble in front of her as they pushed through its sharp tangle. The bramble grew thicker, the light dimmer. Dinah thought she heard water. Dinah pricked her hand on one of the thorns and watched her blood pool in her palm.

"Wardley . . ."

"We're almost there. It's just around here." Wardley stepped to the left and disappeared behind a wall of thorns. Her hands out in front of her, Dinah pressed on. She followed Wardley's footprints until they led her out to a small, magical clearing. Behind them was a silent blue pool of water, so still and clear that the light reflecting from it cast turquoise waves across Wardley's handsome face. At the center of the pool, unattached to any rock or other structure, a waterfall flowed *up* from the middle, its stream turning into mist once it hit a certain height. The mist then spiraled and disappeared into the sky. They stood in silence for a few minutes before Wardley spoke softly as Dinah stared in fascination.

"Incredible, isn't it?" Wardley pulled off his boots and soaked his feet in the shallow pool. Dinah followed his lead. "I've never felt water this clean. It's the perfect temperature— not too hot, not too cold. I found this while you were sleeping off the hallucinations. Cheshire was watching you, and I couldn't just sit there wondering if you would ever wake up, so I wandered." He shook his head. "I prayed that I could take you here one day, that you would wake up. Dinah, think about it—where does the water come from? There is no visible spring under the surface and yet the water keeps rising. It's a miracle."

A smile crept over his face, so lovely that it hurt her heart. "Wonderland is a pretty wondrous place, wouldn't you say? I had no idea that so much lay outside the palace walls. It makes me want to climb on Corning and just disappear."

His eyes followed Dinah as she pushed herself into the pool and waded toward the middle until she stood right before the waterfall. She reached her hand out. Streams of warm water flowed upward through her fingers, as if Dinah herself was the source of this wonder. The water seemed to have a mind of its own between her fingertips, and tiny droplets crawled from the bottom of her wrist to her fingers before lifting off into the sky. She walked back to the edge of the water and climbed out, the hem of her tunic soaked. Smiling, she sat beside Wardley and dipped her wiggling toes into the pool. She glanced over at him, lounging easily beside her on the bank. This was how it always was: Dinah and Wardley. Together. She poked him.

"Remember that summer you stole the tarts from the kitchen, when Harris chased us down the hallway screaming? I've never laughed so hard. You had flour all over your face, and yet when he saw you, the first thing you did was scream 'I didn't do it!'" She laughed at the memory—Wardley, a lanky young boy, his face covered with jam and powder, stuffing as many tarts as he could into his pockets. The sun had filtered through the red heart windows as his thin body tore through the castle, Heart Cards and Harris bellowing behind him, and Dinah too, always a few steps behind, watching him with adoration. Together they hid in the courtyard behind her mother's white rosebushes that snaked over the walls, stuffing their faces with the tarts and giggling uncontrollably.

"It wasn't like you were starving. You just wanted to steal something."

"I did. I was a good kid, but at that moment, stealing tarts seemed dangerous, like a crime punishable in the Black Towers." He grinned. "It was infinitely exciting."

Dinah shuddered at the memory of the Towers and looked down at the pool. "When I'm queen, I will tear them down, until not even the roots remain."

"You have always been fond of making grand queenly statements." Wardley smiled as he tucked her black braid behind her ear. Then a profound sadness pierced his gaze. "It will never be good like this again, will it? War is coming, and somehow you and I are right in the thick of it."

Dinah nodded and stared at the waterfall, completely aware of Wardley's hand resting mere inches away from hers on the bank. She watched a pink fish swim up the waterfall, its tiny fins flapping in the miraculous stream. Suddenly realizing what was happening, the fish reversed course and struggled to swim against the current. It was no use. With a tiny plop, the fish was sucked up into the sky with the water. Wardley continued on, unfazed.

"You know what I keep thinking about? How I hope that my parents have the good sense to stay out of the fight. My mother will stay huddled inside with the rest of the court, holed up in the Great Hall, but my father might just decide to be a hero and don his Card armor for one last battle."

Dinah gave his hand a squeeze. "He won't. He'll know it's you coming."

She wasn't entirely sure she was telling the truth.

Wardley swallowed. "Yes, but . . . what if he doesn't? What if he puts on a helmet, and I don't recognize him on the battlefield? What if I . . . ?" His words faded on his tongue. A few moments passed as they both remained silent. "What are you afraid of?" he whispered.

Dinah took a breath before lowering her voice to a murmur. "Everything. I'm afraid that the men will see that I am just a girl who was rejected by the king. I'm afraid I'll die silently and quietly, like the flame blown from a match, and I'll be nothing more than a child who played at war. I'm afraid of losing you, or Sir Gorrann, or even Cheshire. I'm afraid of letting down the Yurkei people." Dinah lifted her foot and watched droplets of water roll off her muscular calf. "Mostly I'm afraid that I'll die, and it won't matter if I have a crown on my head or not. I'll die the same as other men, with a bloody sword through my chest, one final breath lost in the madness."

A sword. What had the Caterpillar said to her? "You will pierce the heart of one man and . . ."

Her memory was there, but then it was gone again, the way a butterfly would land on her hand but leave the moment she glanced at it. "I'm even afraid of what happens if we are victorious. I'll be queen. Can I rule? Will I be a good ruler or a terrible one like my . . . ?" She stopped. "Like the King of Hearts. If that even happens. If we can get through the gates."

Wardley absently clasped her hand in his, their palms slick with comingled sweat.

"Do you believe we can win, Wardley?"

He stared out at the small pond. His face was ruddy and flushed from the walk, and for a moment he reminded Dinah of the boy with the stolen tarts. But then she saw the stubble creeping up his cheeks and the way his sculpted muscles tensed under his shirt. He had become a man since she had seen him last. He sighed and rubbed his face with his other hand.

"We can win, but it's not in our favor as it stands right now. The king has us outnumbered almost two to one. The iron walls are perfectly round, which means that to surround them, we will be stretched thin in all places. We have the Spades, which will help, for they are ruthless in battle, but he has the Heart Cards, who are the most-skilled fighters in Wonderland. He has Xavier Juflee." He gave a laugh. "We have an exiled princess, the king's Hornhoov, an army of wild natives, and the Spades. And even if we win, once we are inside the gates, the people of Wonderland Palace will not welcome us with open arms. They loathe you, do you realize that? The people fear you, Dinah, and for good reason. You are bringing death and war upon this city, a city that has never seen a battle. Almost every man in the kingdom is a Card, and the king will deploy all of them in his defense."

"Yes, but we have the Yurkei . . ."

"The Yurkei have never attacked a city. What do they know of walls and Iron Gates and a palace made of stone and glass? The mounted Heart Cards will smash against the Yurkei on the north side, while we battle our way through a sea of Hearts, Clubs, and Diamonds, all while the Fergal family rain arrows down around us." Dinah had forgotten about the famous Fergal archers.

Wardley shook his head. "If we are captured, our fate will be much more terrible than dying quickly on the battle-field. They will throw us into the Black Towers to rot, until we become one with the tree or worse. The King of Hearts is a hateful man." He looked over at Dinah, his brown eyes gazing with adoration and sadness on her drawn face. "I swear to you this day, here in this place, that I will kill you before I let the king torture you. And I hope you will do the same for me."

Dinah smiled back at him, knowing that she would never be able to take Wardley's life. No, not even to save him. Love had made her impassively hard and needlessly soft at the same time.

"I keep thinking," he muttered, "that this might be the

last time I do anything. The last time I eat bread. The last time I dip my foot in a pool. The last time that I get to speak with you as a friend, and not as a commander to his queen. Are we ready for that? Am I still to be your king?"

There was an edge in his voice, a need to share with her. Dinah realized with a ragged breath that their relationship was about to change. Her heart started to gallop within her chest, racing so fast she felt it might explode. Despite all the oxygen running through her veins, she was frozen in place. Wardley seemed oblivious to her discomfort. He leaned back onto the mossy ground, stretching his arms above his head, his words shaping her world.

"Tonight could be the last night that I watch the stars simply to remember my place in this world. Everything that we have can be taken away. It will be taken away for many men that rest in those tents, maybe from you, maybe from me. There is no time to waste."

Dinah felt a fury climbing up through her chest, only this time it was different. This was a longing, a need, something that felt like falling, like a string was yanking her heart out of her chest. *Toward him, only him, always him.* She was no longer in control—all she could feel was the desire to touch him. The passion crawled up through her until she became its puppet. It moved her limbs, her mind, her lips. She wanted him. She had waited long enough, and had almost lost him once.

"If this is the last time we will be together, then there is something . . . Dinah, what are you doing?"

He was still speaking when Dinah leaned over him, her arms on either side of his body.

Tenderly, she bent over him, her lips brushing his, as gentle and soft as dew drops on a petal. His were warm and moist, and tipped with everything good Dinah had ever tasted. Her red lips dusted across his, feeling his mouth staying painfully still. He lay motionless, frozen. *What am I doing?* Dinah yanked her head back and looked down at him with confusion and hesitation.

Wardley remained perfectly still for a moment, and then he grabbed the back of her head roughly and pressed his lips hard against hers. Dinah gasped at the force with which he kissed her. It was a hungry kiss with more than a hint of anger beneath it. With a grunt, he flipped Dinah onto her

back and leveled his body over hers before he started kissing her again, ever harder, until Dinah felt her lips going
numb. She lost herself in him, tasting the sweet hint of
mint leaves on his tongue, feeling the muscles rippled across
his shoulders as he pressed down against her. A whimper
escaped his lips, falling into her own, hungrily sucked down
into her core. The kisses were delicious and full of pleasure,
and yet, something wasn't right. His weight was too heavy,
his motions too hard. Wardley's hands were pressed against
her shoulders as if he was holding himself back. His pose
was defensive, his body tensed in anger. As he kissed her
furiously, Dinah felt a wet tear drip down his face onto her
cheek. She pushed his face back. It took her a minute to catch
her breath. This was not how she dreamed their first true
kiss would be—aggressive and accompanied by tears.

"Wardley, what is wrong? What are you doing?" Her eyes
traveled over the face she knew so well, and she could feel
her heart wrench painfully when she recognized his grim
determination. He was forcing himself to kiss her. Dinah felt
the creepings of a familiar dark emotion as she looked up at
the man she loved so much: rejection.

"I'm sorry, Dinah." He turned away from her, his voice shaking. "I can't do this."

Dinah's hands clenched. "What do you mean, you can't do this?"

Wardley sat back and extended his hand to help her up. Dinah slapped it away. "Please don't touch me." She sat up, her limbs trembling with unfulfilled passion.

This couldn't be happening. No.

"Dinah!" Wardley grabbed her roughly, his hands on the sides of her neck, his forehead pushed up against hers. His voice was filled with desperation. "Don't you understand? I *want* to love you this way. I've never wanted anything as much as I want to love you in this way, the way you love me. I've begged and pleaded with the gods to give me those feelings for you! I want to be your king, your husband, your lover. But I cannot . . ." He struggled with the words. "I can't force myself to feel those things for you, no matter how much I wish it."

"You don't mean it. I can't . . ." Her voice trembled.

Wardley jerked backward, and the look of devastation in his eyes shattered her hopeful, delicate heart.

Dinah finished. "I can't lose you too."

Wardley cringed.

"You are my best friend, a part of me! I will fight for your right to rule to my death! Does that mean anything?" His face was contorted in agony as he looked into her black eyes. "Dinah, please say something. I can't bear the silence."

They were both breathing heavily now. Dinah stared at him, her heart falling, spilling like blood down her chest, pouring out from her feet, seeping into the ground. The world was cracking, reassembling itself into dark, jagged places.

"Dinah, please say something. I can't bear the silence."

Her eyes were opened anew.

"Do not speak to me."

Dinah felt a ripping that was both parts of her soul and her vision of their future. It was like being plunged into icy waters when you were burning hot. She was left empty, drained—without her love, without him. . . . *He would never be hers.*

She couldn't breathe. She couldn't bear to look at his beautiful face for another second.

He didn't want her.

"Please leave." She turned away from him, her voice flat and dead. "Please leave, Sir Wardley. You have done your duty here."

He grabbed her arm and tugged it. "Don't turn away from me. I won't leave you, not in this state. Please, look at me."

She turned to him, her face a grimace of stone. "Is this all a game, Wardley? One more secret of my twisted upbringing? Did someone hire you to make me love you? Do you remember that day under the Julla Tree, when you kissed me? Was that part of the plan?"

Wardley grabbed her hands. "There was no plan. You were always my plan, but I can't . . . make myself want you, not in that way. And of course I remember the Julla Tree. I kissed you because I *wanted* to. Because you were the first girl that I ever cared for. But even then, I knew that my feelings for you were not of that nature, no matter how much I tried to force them."

"Force them? Did you force yourself to play with me when we were children? Did Cheshire put you up to it? Or to seek me out when we were older? Were you forced to train me on the sword or to follow me here?"

Wardley shook his head angrily. "No. Never! You're not listening. You don't understand. Dinah, I would do anything for you!"

"Except truly love me in the way a man should love a woman," she replied coldly. "Except kiss me."

"Does that even matter?"

Dinah let out a hysterical laugh. "Does that matter? Does it matter?" She bent over, shallow prickly laughs tearing her into pieces. "It was the only thing that ever mattered, Wardley."

Wardley closed his eyes and whispered to her, his words drifting off in the wind, blowing away with every light dream she had ever had. "*I am yours in every other way . . . you are my best friend . . . my queen.*"

She couldn't listen anymore to his words. Not when her heart was thumping on the ground, bleeding, dying. Tears were flooding her vision, and a retching sob was making its way up her throat. She took a deep breath. "I need you to leave. Now, Wardley."

"Dinah, no—"

"I COMMAND IT!" she screamed at the top of her lungs. "OBEY ME!"

He turned away from her, making his way to the edge of the clearing. "I'll be waiting for you tomorrow morning as we ride north."

She shook her head, holding back the cruel words that longed to drip from her tongue.

Wardley turned back to her for a moment, his face wrenched with guilt before he finally disappeared into the bramble.

Dinah waited until she couldn't hear his footsteps, then collapsed into gut-wrenching tears. An empty hopelessness overtook her, and she lay beside the pool, barely breathing through the ache. The thought of being with Wardley had kept her alive all those cold nights in the Twisted Wood, all those warm afternoons in Hu-Yuhar. She had always envisioned him sitting on the throne beside her, his hand in hers as they led Wonderland into a glorious and peaceful future. Now there was nothing, only blackness and despair. What would she fight for? What would she live for?

Waves of anguish and rejection washed over her, and she let herself drown, glad to feel anything against the numbness that threatened.

She thought of his face, and how just moments ago, his lips had been on hers. She bit down on them so hard that she tasted blood.

For hours, Dinah lay beside the pool, her heart throbbing over each word he had said.

He didn't love her. He never would. He never did.

She was undone.

When the night finally settled around her, she heard someone calling her name. *Wardley?* She listened again. *No. Sir Gorrann.* With trembling hands, Dinah pushed herself to her knees and splashed the clear water of the pool on her face. Opening her black eyes, she stared at herself, hardly recognizing the face in the reflection. She had left Wonderland Palace an idealist, a naive girl who dreamed of an easy crown and ruling beside a man who would understand and love her heart.

Now a jilted woman stared back at her, a forgotten child, a bitter warrior. The ends of her long black hair, her mother's hair, dripped in the pool. *Her mother.* Even when her mother had everything—a crown, a husband, children, and all the riches of Wonderland Palace—she had still been unhappy. But unlike Dinah, at least her mother had had the man she loved. Dinah wouldn't even have that. She was alone. Hands clenching with rage, Dinah picked up her dagger. With two short tugs, she was able to cut off most of her hair, so that it hit her right at the chin. Without a second thought, Dinah tossed her braid into the pool and turned to meet Sir Gorrann. He ran up to her, his eyes filled with concern, his voice raining curses down on her that she didn't hear. The pain was still alive inside her, consuming and insatiable.

The Spade gave her a hard shake, and Dinah's glassy eyes finally connected with his.

"Yer Majesty! Dinah! What's happened?"

Her lips trembled into an ironic smile. "He doesn't want me. After all this time."

Sir Gorrann's eyes filled with sympathy, and he let Dinah lean against him. "I'm sorry, Yer Majesty. He's a bloody fool. Come on, let's get you back to your tent."

She felt raw inside, stripped, and she followed without

thought. Only the anger was left behind, and it was a raging current, Dinah helpless in its flow. She let Sir Gorrann help her through the bramble back to where Morte waited for her. He pawed the ground impatiently until she mounted him.

With a click of her tongue, they were flying over the landscape, leaving Sir Gorrann trailing far behind. With each pound of Morte's hooves, she felt her sadness turning to anger. Her rage was boiling over, spilling out until she seethed with fury. She clutched Morte's mane, driving him harder, faster, until the two of them moved over the earth in a blur of blackness. Disjointed thoughts began to twist in her mind, shadowy tendrils of skewed reason.

A dark smile crept across her face as she let the rage she had held back for so long consume her.

If she could not quench the fire burning within her, she would set Wonderland ablaze.

THE BLACK TOWERS

Water dripped down from a small, rotted hole in the ceiling, trailing down the stone walls and into a tiny rivulet between two roots. The harmonic sound of the water was soon interrupted by a scream, spiraling up from the depths of the Towers. Harris shuddered, his shudder leading to a coughing fit that racked his ribs and left him heaving. Shackles of iron slinked across the floor as he made his way toward the tiny little puddle in his cell. His ancient fingers, once used to turn the pages of glorious books of history and language now struggled to fold a tiny piece of paper that a guard had dropped earlier. It was nothing, just a wrapper, but here in the Towers, an unexpected gift.

"Curses!" he mumbled out loud. There was no reply, not from another prisoner, not from even a guard. A voice would have been so welcome, even if it were full of menace.

He focused back on the task at hand, consoling himself with his own voice. "Remember, my dear, it's not the size of the paper, but the size of your skill that matters." He folded the top of the paper down until the edges aligned with the bottom of the paper and his withered fingers creased it. He continued to work, licking his dry lips from time to time as he struggled to remember what he had taught her all those years ago.

He remembered her sitting in the crook of a tree as he tried to teach her history, rolling her dark eyes and fiddling with the bark. "Harris, how long is forever?" she had asked.

Harris had smiled. "Sometimes, just one second."

He folded the paper wings down so that they were

perpendicular to the body, crest, and tail, and then with a final flourish, he creased the head. Harris smiled and held his creation up in the waning light of the Towers before setting it down in the dirty puddle of water. The crane stared back at him, bobbing slightly.

The queen was coming. He knew it. That was not the question.

The question was who would she be when she got here.

ACKNOWLEDGMENTS

In every novel, there is a point where the author must bridge the cavernous gap between the magical, bright-eyed beginning of the novel and the exciting, steely-eyed ending. I remember feeling inadequate as I moved into what would turn out to be the second novel in the Queen of Hearts series, wondering if I could connect the beginning to the bloody ending that loomed in my future.

This novel was the result of that pressure, but also the unleashing of an imagination that I had pushed away for years because I thought imagining was not something grown-up people did. For too long I ignored it, despised it, and let it manifest itself in other, unproductive ways. When I wrote the Queen of Hearts series, and in particular *Blood of Wonderland*, I let it flow out through every pore. I let it consume me. That is why we have trees that *know*, that is why there are giant stone cranes and curling blue smoke that takes you to the stars. To the readers out there, I hope you hear that imagination isn't just reserved for our fleeting childhoods. It is essential to our hearts.

With that being said, another truth I learned is that had it not been for some incredible people (and lots of coffee consumption), I may not have made it through the Queen of Hearts series.

So, please accept my deepest gratitude and thanks to the kindhearted people who made this novel happen. You have the soul of the Yurkei with the determination of the line of Hearts.

Ryan Oakes, for his endless feedback, support, and the sheer power of his belief in this novel—thank you for your unflagging love, your creative mind, and your amusing nerd knowledge; I'll never stop needing it.

For Maine . . . I wrote this book when you were nothing more than the brightest dream. Now that you're here, I know that even my imagination couldn't fathom something as awesome as you are.

Tricia McCulley and Ron and Denise McCulley, thanks for always coming to the book signings and pretending like it's the first one in all of history. I feel it's important to note here that my own father is a very nice man who has never tried to kill me, not once.

Cynthia McCulley, getting to be your sister never gets old. Thanks for agreeing to be a horse.

To my village, my beloved people who help my writing process by just being their superb selves: Kimberly Stein, Katie Hall, Nicole London, Butch and Lynette Oakes, Karen Groves, Emily Kiebel, Sarah Glover, Cassandra Splittgerber, Elizabeth Wagner, Erin Burt, Amanda Sanders, Katie Blumhorst, Erin Chan, and the entire group hug that is RSLC.

For the beta readers who helped sculpt Queen into something very unique and special—Michelle Rehme, Erika Bates (equestrian fact-checker), Jen Lehmann, Patty and

Sarah Jones, Angela Turner, Holly Cameron, and Stefanie Feustal—thank you. I wish I could take you on a tour of the wood you helped build. We (probably) wouldn't die.

This book and all the Queen novels have passed through the hands of more than a few skilled editors: Erin Armknecht, Jeni Miller, Jess Riley, and Wayne Parrish, who prepared it for the devoted PR team at Sparkpress: Crystal Patriarche, Heidi Hurst, Sara Divello.

To Emilia Rhodes, my editor at HarperTeen, whose skilled and merciless brain is only matched by her generous smile—thank you for putting faith in a book that thought its run complete and giving it a completely new life. I have been dazzled by what you and your team can do. I'm so thankful that Queen found her forever home at HarperCollins.

To Jen Unter, my agent, who was making deals for me before I was even her client, thank you for your dedication, your straightforward nature, and your patience. "Why, sometimes I've believed as many as six impossible things before breakfast."

To the team at HarperCollins: Jenna Stempel, for a cover that makes me happy every time I look at it, and

Reuben Ireland, for the images of Dinah that have come to define her character as much as I have; Gina Rizzo, such a cool chick and such an incredible publicist, and Elizabeth Ward, who is so kind even when she's telling me to be better at Twitter; Alice Jerman, for additional editing and proofing, Jennifer Klonsky, and Jon Howard.

For all the Bookstagrammers who have posted such beautiful pictures of *Queen of Hearts* and now *Blood of Wonderland*—you're my favorite thing.

Thank you finally to a God who promises not a comfortable life but a grace-fueled, fulfilling one. I'm almost halfway through my journey here and I think I'm finally starting to understand the difference.

Read them all!

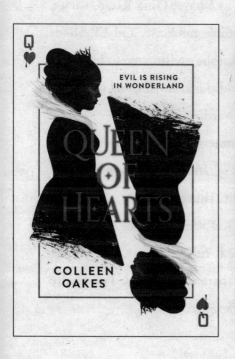

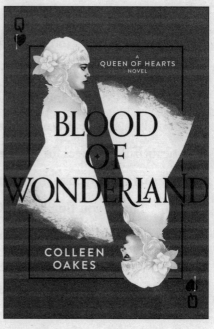

ONLY QUEENS WITH HEARTS CAN BLEED.